A Mod's Story

A Novel by Kris Gray
Loosely based on a screenplay by
Steven M. Smith and Christopher Jolley

To Leah
Enjoy!

Kris Gray

1

First published as a Kindle 2019

First paperback edition 2020

Front cover design by Terry Rawlings

The March of the Mods

Imagine, if you can, a mile long stretch of beach littered with debris, and strewn with moaning bodies lying bloodied and wounded.

No, it's not Normandy France 1944, but Brighton England almost twenty years to the day later. To the holiday makers on that Whitsun weekend in 1964, it must have seemed like a totally new invasion had taken place on the beaches of the popular South England coastal resort.

Fierce fighting had also broken out at other seaside towns as Gangs of Mods and Rockers descended on Clacton and Margate, but the majority had seemingly converged on the seaside town of Brighton.

A considerable number of Mods had arrived either by scooter or train, mostly from London. When they reached the promenade and pier they encountered a not so large contingent of leather clad Rockers idling around planning to enjoy what little entertainment early 1960s Brighton had on offer. It was estimated that by mid-day over one thousand youths had arrived looking for fun but found, (and started) nothing but trouble.

The town, promenade and beach front was also packed with hundreds of elderly out of towners, day-trippers and young families. Now Brighton in 1964 was a far cry from the thriving trendy popular destination it is today, especially for people from London and the east southern counties. However; these were the days well before the average English family ever dreamed of taking a package holiday abroad. They were yet to discover the pleasures of jetting off to sunnier and warmer climates, to places such as the south of France, Spain, and Italy or (unthinkably) even further afield. It was a time before most households, (certainly the working-class ones) had something as basic as a plumbed in bath, or even an indoor toilet. A personal telephone was never considered a necessity nor even an option, indoor heating was coal fires, and a car was almost completely out of the question. So therefore, families would look forward to escaping the drab and foggy grey inner cities, and let the train take the strain. Loaded down with packed lunches, thermos flasks, buckets, spades and wind breakers they'd head excitedly to their nearest pebbly seaside resort. Nevertheless, by the early to mid-sixties the times they were a changing and with the advent of the hire-purchase (HP) incentive, most of the countries youth had moved with it. They were now overall, far more mobile than their parents' generation. Scooter, and to some lesser degree motor bike sales, were at a record high, as teenagers began to realize and enjoy the freedom of independent travel and the joys of the open road. Now no place was inaccessible and Brighton, it seemed, was possibly one of their most popular choices. Well certainly by Londoners, and on this particular not so sunny bank holiday weekend! The place was heaving.

At around noon large gangs of Mods and Rockers had gathered at the Palace Pier where they began jeering and gesturing at each other. When the police arrived, on horseback and with dogs, in an effort to move them on, the gangs staged a mass sit down. After a relatively short space of time and with boredom setting in, factions broke away from each side and the inevitable street fights and running battles began. This soon escalated into all-out bloodshed as many of the protagonists had (it was reported) come prepared for the dust up and were armed with a variety of weapons.

These included bicycle chains, coshes and knuckle dusters, and apparently even knives. Those who hadn't thought to bring an armament, improvised and made wooden staves from smashed up deckchairs for hire. What few deckchairs that weren't appropriated as weapons, were later set on fire.

As the two groups fought on the beach a constant hail of pebbles rained down maiming many on both sides as well as terrified day trippers and families alike.

The Brighton clashes raged on over the entire two-day bank holiday weekend, even moving along the coast to Hastings. Here the pitched battles were imaginatively dubbed by the press as the 'Second Battle of Hastings'. When the fighting eventually stopped, the cost of damage done to shops, cafes and other properties all along the coast was estimated as amounting to tens of thousands of pounds.

Disturbing pictures of perturbed and horrified holiday-makers, many protecting small children, were printed on the front pages of every daily tabloid showing them trapped in the middle of the violent melee.

Many of the youths were taken to hospital with various injuries which did indeed include some knife wounds. It was reported that one Mod was even thrown through a shop front window causing serious lacerations.

There were over a hundred arrested and mostly fined in hastily held court hearings. All pleaded guilty to a succession of offences before being released. Those accused of the more severe wrongdoings later received custodial sentences.

Although there were to be later bank Holiday skirmishes between the rival mobs, it was the Brighton brawl that was later memorialized in the 'cult classic' film 'Quadrophenia' based on the influential concept album written by Pete Townshend and performed by Mod heroes 'The Who.'

Back in 1964 England, post Beat-Nik, jazz types and the Teddy Boy hysteria, the Mods and Rockers were the new youth movements. They, like the Teds before them, were distinct and instantly identifiable teenage rebels. Styling themselves image wise on the music and fashion that influenced them accordingly.

By the mid-sixties you were either a Mod or a Rocker. Mods, aside from loving American soul and R&B music, also grooved to home grown bands like 'The Action', 'Georgie Fame and the Blue Flames', the afore mentioned 'WHO' and (more importantly) street urchins, 'Small Faces', who came from the tough East-End of London.

'Small Faces' were fronted by the widely acknowledged and iconic Mod style setter Steve Marriott who had a voice that defied comprehension and belied his 5 foot nothing white boy stature.

All four of the group were the same height (give or take an inch) and were always impeccably dressed, thanks to a combination of street savvy and dozens of clothes accounts in every trendy outlet in Carnaby Street! Another band the Mods er …tolerated were 'The Kinks' who had a bon-a-fide scooter riding mod in their line-up, bass player Pete Quaife. Mods unanimously hated 'The Beatles' but liked their rivals, the bad boys of R&B the Rolling Stones.

This was best demonstrated when the group was famously left stranded on a podium Centre stage while gangs of Mods rioted at the aptly titled 'Mad Mod Ball'. This event was held at the Empire Pool Wembley and presented by the TV show the Mods had come to claim as their own 'Ready Steady Go'.

Mods adopted, or more accurately created, a smooth sophisticated look wearing sharp, tailor made (short collared) style suits, (Once again on HP) combined with button down or tab collared shirts, and desert boots! The more casual American Ivy League preppy college look, was also popular with the introduction of penny loafers and monogramed sweat shirts.

This whole fashion revolution was then all wrapped up in an old green US Army Parka coat, complete (but not mandatory) with a fur lined hood and military insignia. London's Kings Road and Carnaby Street flourished. Mods from all over the country made weekly forays to the many boutiques and outfitters that specialized in the very latest must have variation, on a must have fashion theme.

The British Union Jack flag and the RAF's roundel, were common images sewed on the backs of the Parkas alongside pop art images of Marvel comic super hero The Silver Surfer, and tragic Hollywood legend Marilyn Monroe. To say the Mods influences were wide reaching would be to under play it!

Even the hairstyles were faultlessly styled and cut in line with what (only the coolest) French screen stars were modeling at the time!

However, if it sounds like Mod was an all-male movement, it wasn't! No; Female Mods played a very big part too and had their own style Queens who set trends and standards. Girls like Ready Steady Go presenter Cathy McGowan, designer Mary Quant and Models Patti Boyd, Jean (The Shrimp) Shrimpton and Twiggy. These female icons unquestionably played as big a part as any male star in placing the country firmly at the top of its game, acknowledged worldwide as the leading style capital of the world.

Drugs were widely used within Mod circles, mostly in the form of amphetamines (known as) purple hearts, black bombers and bennies. Benzedrine was something used by bomber pilots in World War Two, enabling them to fly to and from Germany on bombing missions without falling asleep. Mods used them for the less harrowing task of all night clubbing! Hence Cannabis was not so popular due to its capacity to make the user drowsy when all they wanted to do was rave all night.

Transport was the Lambretta or Vespa scooter which were cheaper (HP) and easier to park in the Soho side streets than cars. These were usually customized with the addition of copious amounts of lights and mirrors, whip aerials and car hood ornaments and badges.

They also only required a provisional license to ride at the age of sixteen whereas with a car you needed to be seventeen and pass a test. Plus, with public transport ending early (not that any self-respecting Mod would be seen dead on a bus) they were the ideal way to enable them to go to the clubs until the early hours.

Rockers on the other hand lived a far less fussy lifestyle! Their musical tastes were sourced from the bygone era of the fifties, good ole 'Rock and Roll'. Elvis Presley was still 'The King,' Eddie Cochran, Gene Vincent, Chuck Berry and Jerry Lee Lewis, even the unlikely hero Bill Haley. Although to be fair Hayley almost single handedly ignited the Rock flame in England.

Rockers didn't have a club scene, nor a pub one, well they wouldn't be allowed in to any for a start. So, they made do with either a ballroom event, headlined by some faded star of Joe Brown or Marty Wilde status, or congregated in road side cafés, service areas and around suburban tea huts in places like Blackheath south London or (a Favorite) Box Hill in Surrey.

The origins of the Rockers are traceable back to the early 1950's and are not to be confused with the more colorful and pedestrian Teddy Boys.

Back then they were labelled as 'Ton Up Boys' due to their fondness for pushing their motorcycles to 100mph. This was known as 'Doing a Ton'.

There were many a death reported in the undertaking of this pastime pursuit but seemingly this only added to the adrenaline filled rush. Their bikes, (unlike the Mods Scooters) had to be English made, like the Triumph Bonneville or a BSA Rocket Gold Star and were rarely customized but spotlessly maintained.

They did however personalize their outfits, albeit all in a similar manner. The Rockers prerequisite or requirement heavy leather jacket would be individualized with the addition of studs, chains, sew on patches and badges. Thick leather belts and buckles held up tough leather trousers or black Levi jeans, tucked into calf high motorcycle boots with a pure white scarf completing the look.

In contrast to the Mods, and in a time when crash helmets were not yet compulsory, Rockers fashion was wrought out of the necessity to protect themselves from any injuries caused by coming off their bikes.

It was an image modeled by (and attributed to) Marlon Brando and Lee Marvin in the motion picture 'The Wild One', although this is debatable as the film was banned in cinemas in the UK throughout the 50's.

Rocker chicks would dress in pretty much the same fashion, never seen in skirts and wore their hair in long pony-tails. Drugs were frowned on in favour of beer and were one of the many things they disliked about the Mods.

Mods began to fade out in the mid-sixties and either morphed into suede heads who in turn became skinheads. Or, due to an increase in drug use and the advent of the psychedelic era, became hippies. The Rockers endured a little better, and maybe due to them being forever out of time roared on into the 1970s.

Mods on the other hand were all but extinct by the early 1970s when Glam Rock took over, stormed the charts and embedded itself firmly in the nation's consciousness. Ironically it was ex Mods David Bowie and Marc Bolan who alongside bands like 'The Sweet', and ex suede heads 'Slade' who became the champions of this questionable glittery bravura.

The high street was now stocked out with Satin flares, feather boas and platform boots. Straight legged jeans and trousers wouldn't be seen in public for over a half decade. This it seemed would be the way of the world, until a backlash to this sparkly epoch came with the arrival of Punk!

First out of the traps came 'The Damned' followed promptly by 'The Clash' and those ultimate punk rockers, 'The Sex Pistols'.

The Punk phenomenon although trailblazing and refreshing, only burned brightly for around three years but in its time, it paradoxically paved the way for what became known as the '79 Mod revival! Ushered in by 'The Jam' and followed sharply by bands like 'Secret Affair', 'The Chords' and 'The Purple Hearts'. Sharp suits button down shirts and neat haircuts returned, and hush puppies once again walked along British streets. Scooters came out of parents lock ups and even the odd seaside punch up made the news. No Rockers this time though as this new breed of Mods had a new adversary, a new strain of Skinhead.

Regardless, Mods were well and truly back, and this is where our story starts, well almost.

Any British seaside resort is a miserable place to be on a rainy day in winter and Brighton promenade was no exception on this particular day at the end of January. The rain was coming down like stair rods, slicing through the air and swiftly filling the drains to overflowing. The sheer torrents made what few people were there fight the elements, rushing for any kind of cover. Very few tourists can be found here during the winter months, maybe some day trippers looking for some interesting items in the Lanes but the beach? Forget it. Brighton beach is not the best on the south coast consisting mostly of shingle, not smooth sand. This doesn't stop the town attracting a considerable number of tourists every year, sometimes in excess of 150,000 at weekends in the height of summer, especially from London and the Medway towns.

One of the main attractions is the Palace Pier that took almost eight years to complete and was eventually opened in May 1899 costing £27,000, a phenomenal amount for the time, almost three million in today's money. It was a replacement for the Chain Pier that had been built in 1823 which was due to be demolished but was destroyed by a storm. There was a theatre at the end which hosted summer variety shows until the seventies but was removed in 1986 with plans to replace it. However this has never happened and there are now fairground rides and an amusement arcade in its place. The Palace Pier is a thriving concern, despite the IRA's attempt to blow it up in 1994. A plan thwarted by a controlled explosion by the Army.

There are two piers, well there were two but the Pavilion on the West Pier, which had been closed in 1976, caught fire in 2003 leaving a burnt out shell. Because it is a grade one listed building there have been numerous plans to renovate but it is now a skeleton standing off the coast.

On this day the wind was howling along the pier with not a sole in sight. In fact you could fire a machine gun along the length with no danger of killing anyone. The forecast offered no respite for the next few days, if anything it was expected to get worse with storm conditions. Cross channel ferries were cancelled for the next twenty four hours.

A lone figure sits huddled on a deck chair under the pier with an unlit cigarette in his mouth as he watches a lone walker stumble along the beach with a reluctant dog in tow. He smiles to himself as the woman attempts to instill some joy into the drenched Yorkshire terrier who was showing no sign of wanting to run for the ball she continued to throw for him.

Harry York had turned sixty in November the previous year, most of the old gang, Steve, Frank, Ed and Bernie, had rallied round and bought him more than a few pints of Guinness in The Fiddler's Elbow, the Irish Pub on West Street. He barely remembered getting home. Thankfully Steve had booked a taxi and prepaid the driver as Harry probably didn't have enough readies to cover the trip. It had been over five years since ill health had forced him to retire early from his job as a bus driver. Suffering from sleep apnea meant that he could fall asleep at the wheel at any time, not good for someone driving a bus full of passengers. Now money was too tight to mention, his company pension had just kicked in but his private one had five more years to run.

Harry wasn't a natural son of Brighton, he had originally been born in Poplar, east London but his parents had moved to Lewisham in south London when he was only four. His father moved from job to job often finding himself unemployed leaving his mother to do as many cleaning jobs as she could in a week. She was forced to take on more when her husband suddenly walked out on his family. This left her struggling to bring up her only child who was only eleven at the time.

It would be many years, much water under the bridge and a life changing incident that brought Harry to Brighton.

But for now..........

The woman with the dog gradually grew smaller as she and Fido shuffled along the beach towards what was left of the West pier. Harry was envious of her, at least she had someone who loved her, even if it was a soggy doggy. Harry smiled to himself at his expression 'soggy doggy' rubbing his two day beard growth absent mindedly. He then moved his fingers up his age lined face to the jagged scar that ran millimeters from his left eye round the lobe of his left ear. Instantly the memory of getting it flashed vividly into his mind, shrugging his shoulders as a shiver ran down his spine he forced himself to erase it.

'Happy days, happy days.' He mutters softly to himself. 'Fuck! That hurts!' He exclaims as he rubs his jaw again sending the pain from his tooth shooting up the side of his head. 'Gotta go see the bloody dentist, yeah, happy days.'

With more than a little effort, he manages to lift himself out of the deck chair. Still with the unlit cigarette in his mouth, he pulled himself up to his full height, stretching his damaged back. Three vertebrae at the base of his spine were missing the discs and had welded together. Despite the heavy pain killers he took constantly the pain was there 24/7.

After removing the cigarette and replacing it in the packet Harry pulled the hood of his well-worn Parka over his head and tightened it. Forcing his hands into the pockets he proceeded to make his way from under the pier into the rain that instantly drove into his face, to make his way up the beach to the promenade. With the rain still making its full frontal assault on his face he made his way about 200 yards until coming to a small café just off the prom. He stopped outside for a few moments to peer through the window, breathed a heavy sigh, and then pushed the door open.

There are no customers inside, just a pretty young girl of around eighteen years old with long blonde hair looking completely bored chewing on some gum whilst looking at a newspaper. It's a typical British seaside café with gingham table cloths and condiments on each one. A radio was playing music so low that the tune was not instantly recognizable, Harry doubted he would know it anyway having lost interest in the charts over twenty years ago. As he steps inside the girl looks up from her paper.

'Oh, hi Harry, long time....'

'Hello Sara, busy day?'

'Wouldn't you know it, just when I was hoping for an early one.' Harry smiled.

'Is she in?'

'Out the back, hang on I'll give her a shout.'

Sara disappeared through the bamboo curtain, there's some clattering of saucepans and muffled swearing. In no time Sara re-emerges from the kitchen with another woman hot on her heels holding a frying pan and dishcloth in her hands.

'For crying out load Sara are you not able to do something for yourself?'

The angry look on her face quickly changes to a smile when she sees Harry standing at the counter.

'Harry! So good to see you, come here.'

'Good to see you too Rita.'

Rita comes around to the front of the counter to throw her arms around his neck, still holding the pan and dishcloth, to kiss him on the cheek.

'Get your coat off and sit down, it's nice and warm in here.' Harry does just that. 'What can I get you, the usual, black coffee, and no sugar?'

'Sounds just right.'

'And I bet you could do with a bacon sarnie.'

'Ah, not sure I can stretch to one of those.'

'Harry, come on, we don't need your money here,' Rita looks down at the floor, 'I'm sorry I missed your birthday bash.'

'No worries, I don't remember much about it anyway.' They both laugh, 'I was hammered.'

'Well that makes a change.' Quipped Rita which brought on more laughter. 'Guinness was it?'

'Ha, ha, yes it was.'

Rita goes back around the counter to the coffee machine, Sara is standing there smiling. Rita looks at the time, then out of the window, sighs and looks back at Sara.

'Go home love, there's not much going on here today so I'll probably close up early.'

'OK, will I still get paid?' Rita chuckles, opens the till and takes out a twenty pound note which she presses into the girl's hand whilst shaking her head and snarling with a smile.

'Go on, I'll see you tomorrow.'

'Thanks Reet.' Sara goes out the back to collect her hat and coat. ''Bye Reet, 'bye Harry, see you again.'

'You still seeing that fella working up on the dodgems?' Harry asks.

'Nah, all he wanted was to get inside me knickers.' Harry and Rita both laugh.

'That's what they all want.' Harry and Rita say in unison.

'I live in hope of finding one who doesn't.'

'Good luck with that.' Harry laughs again, Sara shrugs her shoulder, mouths goodbye and flounces out the door.

'She's a good kid Reet.'

'Yes she is, can't really afford her on days like this but I don't want to lose her either.'

'You won't, she thinks the world of you, you're her surrogate mother, that real one of hers, the alkie, is a waste of space, and the father? Don't get me started on him.'

'Yeah I know, I know, I'm thinking about asking her to come and move in with me.'

'You should, it would be good for both of you, how's business anyway?'

'On days like this?' Rita sweeps her arm around the empty room. 'Bustling, but on good days I need more than Sara. On the whole I'm keeping my head above water, just.'

Harry nods in understanding, Rita turns on the coffee machine then goes out the back to start frying some bacon for Harry's sandwich. Harry sits staring out of the window watching the few people braving the elements. An old lady, making her way to the bus stop, has an umbrella ripped out of her hand by a sudden gust of wind to fly away towards the sea. Realising she has no hope of recovering it the woman makes her way to the bus shelter, sits and starts to cry. Harry wishes he could go and help her but also knows there is no hope of saving it.

'Bloody awful out there!' Rita shouts from the kitchen as if reading Harry's thoughts.

'Certainly is and the forecast is not looking any better.' Harry shouts back, 'Still, it's lovely when the sun comes out.'

'That won't be for a while.' Rita replies as she comes back through the bamboo curtain with Harry's sandwich. 'It's January and it's England.'

''Nuff said.' Harry chuckles, Rita puts the sandwich down and sits in front of Harry. He tucks into it with relish as if he hadn't eaten for days. As he takes a second bite he winces with pain. 'Ahh!'

'What's wrong?' asks Rita.

'Toothache still.'

'What? You've had that for months, I told you the last time I saw you, when was it, October?'

'Yeah, yeah, yeah, I know but I hate dentists.'

'Who doesn't? It's not going away though, it'll just get worse. What's better, half an hour of pain and discomfort in the dentist's chair or weeks and weeks of it? I bet its awful eating isn't it?'

'Yeah, tend t'stick to soup and anything sloppy, and bacon sarnies.'

'Well unless you get something done, and soon, there's no more bacon sarnies here for you.' With that she punches him playfully on the shoulder. 'Kapish?'

'Yeah, kapish. Actually I've got an appointment tomorrow morning.'

'You're not just saying that to safeguard the supply of bacon sarnies are you?' Harry laughs.

'As if.'

'Hmm, as if.'

'No, seriously, it's been getting too much so I'm biting the bullet tomorrow.'

'Sure you can do that with a bad tooth?' They both laugh. In the background 'In the City' by the Jam comes on the radio. Rita jumps out of her seat and turns the radio up full blast. 'C'mon, let's dance.'

'I'm a bit old for that.'

'Never too old to dance honey.' She comes back to Harry and drags him out of the chair. Together they dance around the tables, laughing and singing along with the song.

'DAHDA, DAH, DAH, DAH, DAH, DAH! IN THE CITY! 'They sing the chorus in unison laughing, Harry stops before the song is finished easily out of breath and slumps back into his chair.

'I told you I'm too old for this.' Harry laughed as he said it while Rita continued to dance until the track finished then turns the radio down when the next song, a ballad, came on.

'You should dance more often, get yourself fit, you're out of shape you old bugger.'

'Only if you dance with me.' Harry said whilst still gasping for breath. 'They don't write them like that anymore do they?'

Rita sits back down as well.

'You're right there.'

'Good old Ken Bruce, I like his show, this new stuff, it's called R&B, how can they call it that? R&B is Chuck Berry and Eddie Cochran, stuff like that not B-bloody-yonce! They all sound the bloody same.' Harry laughs out loud. 'Listen me, I've successfully turned into my old man. That's what he used to say about the Jam.'

'Mine too, those were the days.' They gaze into each other's eyes without speaking again for a few moments. 'What are you going to do for the rest of the day?'

'Meeting the gang for a few bevvies.'

'I thought you didn't have enough money for a sandwich?' Harry looked sheepishly away from Rita. 'Hey, I'm only kidding, of course beer is more important than food.' Harry chuckled and stood up to put his coat back on.

'I hope business picks up Reet.'

'It will Harry, it will. Rule Britannia eh?'

'Yeah, Rule Britannia.'

Rita puts her arms around him and they hug each other, holding on for the best part of a minute until they finally pull apart.

'Don't be a stranger Harry.'

'I won't, especially if you make bacon sarnies like that.'

They both laugh, hug one more time, then Harry turns to leave, looking back at Rita before opening and going through the door.'

'Bye Harry.' She whispers to herself when the door closes.

2.

After he closed the door to Rita's café, resisting the urge to look back, Harry turned left towards the pier. The wind was dropping and the rain easing off. He was on a mission, the time was close to four o'clock and getting dark, with the best part of two miles to go it was going to be completely dark by the time he arrived at his destination, which he did by four thirty.

Brighton Borough Cemetery lies off the Lewes Road, by the time Harry arrived the rain had almost stopped and it was very dark. That didn't matter to Harry, he could find his way through the tombstones blindfolded. Within five minutes he arrived at his destination to kneel down in front of a small gravestone. With a sigh he reaches out and runs his right index finger over the name engraved in the stone. Tears start to well up in his eyes so he gropes in his pocket for a tissue. When he can't immediately find one Harry wipes away the tears with the back of his hand.

'Miss ya.' Was all he said as he stood up to leave.

3

Rita watched Harry as he walked along the street until he disappeared around the corner.

'The pub's the other way Harry,' she sighs heavily, 'guess I know where you're going.'

She drops the latch on the lock and turns around the sign to say closed. Rita goes back around the counter to turn out the lights leaving just the one in the kitchen on then goes to a cupboard in there. Here she finds a small bottle of vodka that she takes to pour a generous amount into a tea cup.

'Cheers Harry, say hello from me and tell him I miss him too.' She then takes a swig from the cup and coughs as the fiery liquid burns in her throat. 'Bloody fire water.' She exclaims as she goes to take another hit then reaches into her handbag for her cigarettes. 'Yeah Harry I've given up as well!' laughing as she says it.

Rita pours another vodka as she lights a cigarette, sits down and closes her eyes whilst inhaling deeply on it. A feeling of sadness washes over her, it was always hard to see Harry these days, a mere shadow of his former self.

'If he doesn't do something about that bloody tooth I'll take a pair of pliers to it myself.' She chuckles at the thought.

Rita Hanson was a year younger than Harry but, unlike him, had grown up in Brighton. She'd been working in the café for almost twenty years, the past five as the owner, when her boss, Tony, died suddenly of a heart attack. Rita didn't know that he had left it to her until his solicitor contacted her. Tony was gay, well who isn't in Brighton, but that didn't stop people thinking Rita and he were an item especially as they were always laughing and joking together. Also he wasn't openly gay, most didn't realise he was, hence the 'item' rumours. Rita had been very upset by his death, she hadn't had a steady relationship herself since, well since a long time. She wasn't particularly sure she wanted one anymore being quite happy with her own company.

She'd put away quite a reasonable nest egg for herself. Tony had also left her a considerable sum of money, as well as investing in a pension for her that was due to mature in two years time. Not to mention Tony's flat, worth a considerable amount in Brighton, which he'd also left her. So the plan was to pack up when she hit sixty, sell the flat, give the café to Sara and head off somewhere warmer than Brighton. Not Spain, everyone went to Spain, there were more Brits there than Brighton, no Malta was top of the list, she'd had a great holiday there back in the day.

'But what will I do about Harry?'

4.

Nobody likes going to the dentist and Harry was no exception. His memories of going when he was a child still weighed heavily on his mind. His mother, who constantly had trouble with her teeth, blamed him for her problems saying she had none until he was born. The family dentist had not been a likeable man, he would constantly go into the next room to puff on a cigarette. The smell and taste of nicotine on the man's fingers as he probed around in Harry's mouth were as real today as if it were yesterday. The sound of the drill would send shivers down his spine and that fear of it slipping and tearing through his cheek just wouldn't go away. As he sat in the waiting room listening to someone being tortured in the next room Harry felt a compulsion to flee the scene. It was only the pain throbbing in his jaw that prevented him from doing so.

The waiting was the hardest part, trying to read one of the ancient magazines, looking over the pages without taking anything in.

'I should have brought a book.' He muttered to himself.

'Sorry did you say something?' An elderly woman, about ten years his senior and the sole remaining patient waiting asked him.

'No, just talking to myself, these mags are so old they predict man landing on the moon before 1970.' The lady, not getting the joke, doesn't respond. 'I was saying to myself that I should have brought a book.'

'Oh, right. Just here for a check-up?'

'No, well, maybe, I've had a raging toothache for weeks now. I hate coming to the dentist but as it refuses to go away I've given in and come here to deal with it, not keen though.'

'I'm the same, I had perfect teeth, no trouble until my son was born then I had nothing but trouble, one extraction after another, most of what I have now are false.'

'Funny, that's what my mother used to say, I'm beginning to wonder if that's what all mothers say to their kids.' The woman makes no comment, 'I hope you're not here to have another one out.'

'What? Oh no I need a new set of dentures, I've lost so much weight they don't fit anymore, if I cough or laugh they fall out.' With that she starts to laugh and her teeth start to come loose causing her to put a hand over the mouth to stop them. 'See what I mean?'

Harry laughs too.

'I've still got all mine, other than my wisdom teeth that is, had those out in one go in hospital when I was twenty five, but this one is really giving me gyp.'

At that moment the tannoy crackled into life,

'Mister York room three please.'

'Oh well,' Harry says 'Over the top!'

'Hope it's not too serious.'

'So do I Miss, so do I.'

'Miss! Those were the days.' She laughs as Harry gets up to leave the room making his way to room three.

'Come in Mister, ah Mister York, sit down.' The dentist indicates the chair which Harry views with dread and hesitates for a few seconds. 'So what's the problem Mister York?' Harry lowers himself into the chair, the dentist tips it back and pulls the light over.

'I've had toothache here for a few weeks now, comes and goes.' Harry indicates where the pain is.

'Okay please open wide.'

Harry opens his mouth as wide as he can, hurting his jaw in the process. The dentist starts to pick at the plaque in between Harry's teeth giving instructions to the young dental nurse at this side. After what seems like an eternity he stops.

'Please rinse.' Thankful for the respite Harry leans over to the mouthwash and does as instructed.

'Is that it?'

'Not yet, are you a smoker Mister York?'

'No, doctor's orders.'

'But maybe now and then?' Harry doesn't deny it. 'When was the last time you went to a dentist? I have no record of you having been to me or this practice before.'

'Er I'm not sure, a couple of years maybe.'

'I thought as much, more like a couple of decades, they're really not in a very good condition, the plaque build-up will take some time to clear and you need a serious deep clean. There is also an inflammation of the gums, more so here.' He pokes the more inflamed spot 'which I think maybe an abscess caused by a rotting to the root, I'll need to take an X-ray to be sure then it will have to come out. In the meantime I'll give you some anti-biotics to reduce the abscess before I can remove that tooth and quite possibly a few more'

'Is that really necessary, I mean if the swelling goes down do you need to pull the tooth?' asks Harry.

'That depends if you are happy for the pain to come back again which it most certainly will if you leave it unchecked, up to you, I'll know more after the X-ray'

'Okay, okay do what you must.'

'Good, once I've taken an X-ray you can make an appointment for me to remove the offending tooth then we can talk about a deep clean.'

'Thanks, I think.'

'Are you on benefits?'

'Yes, job seekers for what it's worth, I'm sixty so employers aren't exactly queuing for my services.'

'Please go with the nurse who will take the X-ray and deal with the paperwork, here is a prescription for the anti-biotics, have a good day Mister York.'

'Hmm, I'll try.'

5.

Having been to the chemist to collect his anti-biotics Harry decides to wait until the next day before he starts the course. This lunchtime he was due to meet up with his old gang of Mods and there would be a few pints sunk as they reminisced about the old days.

Maybe a whisky or two, as well.

His favourite haunt, the venue of his sixtieth birthday bash, The Fiddlers Elbow, was a short walk from the chemist shop. It took him past 'Gigging Guitars' where he stopped to window shop. There was a beautiful Gibson Les Paul Gold Top reissue hanging there for £2,995. Harry stands looking for some time, wishing he could afford to buy it but knowing that he never will. With a heavy sigh he moves to the pub, already almost half an hour late.

When Harry opens the door he sees a trio of his old pals chatting and laughing in their usual corner. The pub has changed a lot over the years especially now that Brighton has become a magnet for the monied gay community. However there was still a pool table at the far end of the room where a couple of spotty youths, probably underage and skipping school, were shooting some pool. Once there had been a public and lounge bar but they had now been morphed into one big lounge. Drinks prices were astronomical due to high rents, business rates and taxes. Somehow the unemployed still managed to find the money to pay them.

''Arry me boy, get your arse over here, there's a pint of Nigerian lager here waiting for ya, where ya been?' Steve Hopkins, Harry's best friend calls out to him, Harry smiles as he makes his way over to them.

'Had to go to the dentist, serious tooth ache.'

'What you need boy is some alcoholic anaesthetic, perhaps I should get you a double whisky as well to rub on your gums or even better a line or two.'

'Maybe later with the whisky as I guess you don't have any Columbian marching powder.'

'I might, I might.' Steve winks at him.

'Yeah right.' Everybody laughs.

'Seriously mate, there's nothing much worse than tooth ache, come on sit down and get this pint down you, you have some catching up to do.' Harry sits down and takes a long sip on his beer.

'How long have you guys been here then?'

'About ten minutes but we're on our third pint.' With that they all burst into laughter.

'So it's a good job I'm late then otherwise I'd have been here twiddling my thumbs until you lot turned up.'

'Or playing with yourself.' Steve jokes.

'Too old for that, don't remember how to.'

'Oh I'm sure you could, given the right incentive like some of the DVDs I've got at home.'

'I'm sure you have.' Harry said sounding unconvinced.

Steve Hopkins was Harry's best friend and had been since they were first placed next to each other at school when they were eleven years old. Along with Frank Dyer, Bernie Coupe and Ed Rawlings they had been inseparable since meeting at The Chase Secondary Modern in Lewisham. They all came from similar working class backgrounds and would all immerse themselves in the Mod music culture of the seventies.

Hopkins sported a full beard which he first grew the day he was released from Borstal at the age of nineteen, some forty years before. He'd spent almost a year there after being caught with a few grams of cannabis, something that would have brought a slap on the wrist these days. The beard, along with the long hair, now in a ponytail, had turned from his previous auburn to a silvery grey.

Bernie played the drums, something he had been taught by his father who played in a jazz band. Being huge fans of The Jam, Harry and Steve picked up guitars which they both quickly learned to play. Together with Bernie they formed a band. Frank and Ed, despite loving the music of the day, weren't interested in learning to play instruments, Frank wanted to be a footballer whilst Ed, whose father ran a betting shop had ambitions of following in father's footsteps.

Sadly Frank's ambitions had been thwarted by his contracting TB when he was twenty which damaged his lungs. Instead of Ed running a booking shop the betting addiction took a hold causing him to lose everything many times over. Today he was conspicuous by his absence.

'So brothers, how's it all hanging?' Harry asks after sinking almost half of the pint of Guinness, 'all fit and well?'

'Where do you want us to start mate? I was at the doc's the other day, having a problem hitting the back of the pan, if you know what I mean?' Steve chips in.

'Is it bad?' Harry asks.

'Oh don't let him get started on the bloody prostate story, we've all heard it, many times over.' Frank laughs.

'There's nothing to laugh about, it kills more blokes than tit cancer kills women but 'coz it's a bloke's thing it gets ignored. If it was a bird's problem there'd be bloody scanners on every street corner!'

'Yeah right but you probably don't have prostate cancer you just you just keep bleating on about having the doc's fingers up your arse.'

'Well how would you like having a finger up your arse?' Steve retorts indignantly.

'Depends on whose finger it is.' Harry chips in.

'I know I wouldn't keep on about it like you do.' adds Frank.

'Keeping on about what?' Bernie looks up from his newspaper where he is checking out the odds on the days races.

'Oh wake up dough boy, Stevie's on about his non-existent prostate cancer.'

'Oh, that daft fucker.' Steve opens his mouth to protest but laughs, the others join in.

'More Beer!' Steve shouts then stands up to go to the bar, 'same again ladies?' Everyone shouts in approval.

'It's good to laugh guys, don't do much of that these days', claims Harry.

'Who does?' Bernie adds grumpily.

'I do!' Frank chips in.

'Good for you' adds Steve.

'What happened to us eh?' Harry askes 'I mean I used to look forward to meeting up with you guys but these days it's getting to be more like a funeral than a party. Anyway, where's Ed?'

'Haven't you heard?' Frank asks, 'he's in hospital, not looking good.'

'Eh! What is it?'

'Cancer, pancreas.'

'No, that's what took my mother, she went from diagnosis to the crematorium in four weeks.' Harry is visibly shocked by the news of his old friend's condition. 'Where is he?'

'The Hospice in Hove.'

'Why didn't anyone tell me?' The three friends fall silent, pick up their beers and start to drink. 'Well?' No one answers him 'Bloody hell! He didn't look well at his daughter's wedding'

'No, he didn't,' Frank replies, they all fall silent again seeking solace in their beers.

'We should go and see him.' Says Harry.

'Why?' asks Steve. 'It's too depressing.'

'He's our friend and he must be feeling like shit.'

'He's got his family around him'

'We're his fucking family as well, what's the matter with you all? We've been friends for fifty fucking years, you're going to abandon him now?'

They all shuffle their feet and drain the last of the beer in their glasses. Harry gathers the empties and takes them to the bar.

'Same again?' the trio mumble agreement. Harry gives the order to the barman and wanders over to the juke box to thumb through the titles, puts a coin in the slot, makes a selection then goes back to the bar. Within a few seconds the Small Faces 'What'cha Gonna Do About it?' comes out over the speakers. Harry turns towards his friends.

'You must be soft in the head Harry, the last thing Ed wants to see are our ugly mugs.' Harry just puts his head on one side then raises his eyebrows without saying a word.

'Ah fuck it! All right, all right you mad bastard.' Steve chuckles, have it your way but don't be surprised if he tells us to fuck off!'

Harry places the fresh beers on the table and smiles.

6.

Harry is drunk, very drunk having lost count of the number of pints of the black stuff he drank. Then there were the whiskies, how many? He didn't suppose he would remember, nor would anyone else. As he stumbled his way down to the front he was still singing the Small Faces tune that he'd played on the juke box what seemed like an eternity ago. With three steps forward and one step back he slowly made his way to the promenade. Despite the cold wind the excess of alcohol managed to shelter him from the storm. The world began to spin as he stumbled across the road, being narrowly missed by a taxi that sounded his horn. Miraculously Harry made it safely to the other side.

With a deep breath he tried, unsuccessfully, to clear his head as he made his way to collapse on a bench overlooking the sea. A tune, one of those great tunes drifted into his mind and he was there, back in the day, when the sun was shining.

7.

This day, in May 1978, is a hot, sunny day, the kind of summers day that we all seem to remember were constantly there when we were children. Why do we always remember the sunny days and not the miserable ones when we couldn't go out to play in the park? When we could only be stuck in the house, maybe a friend was allowed to come in, maybe not. Those days were sad but we don't remember them, do we? No the sun always shone on high days and holidays, when we were kids. In the days before twenty four hour TV and computer games when we had to make our own entertainment. No, the sun always shone when we were kids.

This day was one of them.

Brighton front and beaches are heaving with thousands of people, young and old, laying there, soaking up the sun. It's lunchtime so the pubs are still open, doing a roaring trade in cold beer, lemonade, cola and a multitude of other drinks to cool the body and sooth the throat. Everywhere you look there is an ice cream van with queues too long for some people, especially stressed parents of small children begging for a 'Ninety Nine', a 'Raspberry Ripple' or a simple orange lolly. The Palace Pier was also throbbing with tourists, older people would relax in deckchairs enjoying the breeze off the sea. Teenagers thronged to the fun fair at the end, especially the ghost train where couples could kiss, cuddle and fondle in the dark.

This day brought the young Harry York and his quartet of friends, Steve Hopkins, Frank Dyer, Bernie Coupe and Ed Rawlings from their South London homes to the coastal town. The M23 had been open only a few years when they took to it to head down to the coast and Brighton their eventual destination. As they roared into town on their gleaming scooters they headed for the front and the Marina Drive. The group managed to find a few spots to park, much easier than if they had cars, then rushed to the wall that overlooked Madeira Drive and the sea. Madeira Drive was the final point of the vintage rally from London, immortalised in the 1953 film 'Genevieve'. Fun to watch now, see the route from London to Brighton and the tram lines in London, not to mention the lack of cars.

'Smell that boys.' Steve stands up on the wall, closes his eyes and takes a deep breath.

'Smell What?' Ed mumbles.

'The sea you miserable bastard, the sea.'

'Smells like shit.' Ed replies

'Sure you haven't shit yourself and that's what you can smell?' laughs Steve. 'Does nothing excite you Eddie? Isn't this better than being in Catford on a lovely day like this?'

'Nothing wrong with Catford.' Ed grumbles, 'I could have gone to the dog track instead.' He adds

'Yeah and lost yer shirt, I've never seen a poor bookie, something you should know about.'

'Get off his back Steve,' Harry chips in, 'you know what he's like, why'd you have to keep riding him?'

'I don't know,' Steve closes his eyes, faces towards the sea and the sun then spreads his arms out. 'I can't help myself, he's just so bloody miserable all the time.'

'Just fuck off Steve and leave me alone.' Steve jumps off the wall and puts his arm around Ed's shoulder who makes a half-hearted attempt to shake it off.

'I'm just pulling yer plonker mate, if only you'd lighten up a bit sometimes, maybe, just maybe I wouldn't keep doing it.'

'Lighten up!? With me dad laying in 'ospital with the cancer? Ed then aggressively shakes Steve's arm off his shoulder and storms away.

'Oh, nice one Steve,' Harry turns to him 'well done, don't the words mouth and gear come to mind before engaging?' He goes off after Ed.

'Excuse me!' Steve adds with an air of indignation as Harry turns to face him whilst continuing to walk backwards, narrowing his eyes with a drop dead look. 'All right, all right, I'm sorry!' Harry turns back to catch up with Ed. 'Miserable bastard' Steve mutters to himself.

'Give it up Steve.' says Bernie.

'Yeah he's having a bad time with his dad, how would you feel if it was yours?' Frank asks.

'Elated, I hate my old man.'

'Yeah right, of course you do.'

Harry comes back with Ed who looks away from Steve, the others eyes however bore into Steve's who heaves a heavy sigh.

'I'm sorry mate, I wasn't thinking of your dad, it must be difficult to wrap your head around.'

'It is.'

'Come on I'll buy you a pint.' Ed forces a half smile and nods his acceptance. Together they walk off towards the pier which is just a short distance away.

'Look at all this crumpet!' Gasps Steve. Everywhere they looked there were scantily clad girls lying on the beach, strolling along the pier or the prom, or buying ice cream.

'What about them?' Bernie croaks, trying improve his mood whilst pointing in the direction of a group of girls in bikinis who had just bought some ice cream from the van at the beginning of the pier. 'They are fit.'

'Well fit.' Steve adds.

'Go on then Bernie,' Frank says punching Bernie softly on the arm. 'You're the ladies' man, get in there.'

'You mean he acts like a girl.' Harry says and everyone, including Ed, laughs. Bernie doesn't seem so amused.

'Why don't you go and do all the talking Harry, if you think you're so good.'

'Never said I was,' Harry replies, still laughing.

'Leave it to me, I'll do the talking, the ladies can't resist me.' Steve announces as he pushes his chest out pulling himself up to his full height to strut like a peacock.

'That's all we need.' Ed chips in, 'He thinks he's God's gift to women.'

I AM God's gift to women, just you lot watch this.'

Before anyone can say anything more he saunters over to the girls who turn towards him as he approaches. The boys watch as he starts to make conversation with them. What he says can't be heard but he seems to be charming them.

'Looks like he might be getting somewhere.' Frank observes.

'Trust me,' Harry says wryly, 'it won't go well.'

'Why?' Asks Bernie

'Because he's as subtle as a bomber pilot.' Harry replies. As if to punctuate what he said one of the girls rams her ice cream into Steve's face whist the other kicks him in the shins. The boys burst out laughing.

'Now that,' Ed says through his laughter, 'really has cheered me up.'

8.

'Harry! Harry! Are you all right?' Harry pulls himself out of his reverie to look around for the voice calling him. 'Harry!' he's now sitting on the beach, against the wall, soaking wet from the rain, 'Harry for Christ sake, what are you doing down there?'

He looks up to see Rita above him on The Kingsway.

'I'm fine, a bit wet but fine.'

'Are you sure? You don't look it.'

'Yeah, I think so.' With that he tries to stand up, falls back onto the beach, and tries to get up again.

'Harry, you stupid bastard, what are you doing?' Wait, I'm coming down.'

Rita rushes to the steps, comes down to make her way as quick as she can to Harry who is now kneeling on the beach. As she reaches Harry to try and help him to his feet he throws up splashing her shoes.

'For fuck sake Harry, how did you get yourself in such a sorry state?'

'Had a couple of beers.' Harry grins as he says it.

'A couple, yeah a couple of dozen maybe, come on let's get you to the café.'

Rita wipes the contents of Harry's stomach from her shoes in the sand whilst trying not to gag from the smell herself.

Harry struggles, with Rita's help, to stand up, after which they made their way back up the steps and on to Rita's café. Sara is doing some cleaning in the kitchen. This time there is an elderly couple sitting by the window eating an all-day breakfast, despite the fact that it's late afternoon. Rita drops Harry into a seat as far away from them as possible.

'Don't move, I'll get you an Alka-Seltzer and some coffee.'

'Skip the coffee, just the drugs, thanks.'

The All-day breakfast couple eye him warily, Harry attempts to smile in their direction but fails miserably so looks down to his hands in his lap to avoid their stare. After a few seconds he looks up again.

'Having a nice time in Brighton?' He asks them with a slurred voice.

'Yes.' The man replies, feeling a little awkward, obviously not wanting engage in conversation with a drunk. As Harry was about to push himself a bit further Rita returned from the kitchen to save the couple any further embarrassment.

'Leave my poor customers alone,' she whispers in his ear as she puts the glass with the fizzing liquid down in front of him, 'and drink up.'

Harry raises his glass at the elderly couple.

'Cheers! Here's to a happy holiday.' The man nods and hurriedly continues eating.

'Harry!!' Rita admonishes him.

'Sorry, I'll be a good boy.' With that he snaps off a salute in her direction and downs the mixture in one go, then burps loudly. 'Yuk!'

'Harry, if you can't behave yourself you can go back to sleep on the beach in the rain.'

'Sorry Reet, sorry, not feeling at my best.'

'And whose fault is that?'

'Steve and the boys, I just wanted a couple of pints, say hello and go home to catch up on my housework.' Harry raises his eyebrows with a half-smile towards Rita. 'Besides, I don't really like beer.'

'What about whisky?'

'Ahh, now that's something else, errr...........' Harry shakes his head in the hope of making the room keep still. 'Is that offer of coffee still on?'

'What am I going to do with you?' Rita asks whilst standing up, Harry opens his mouth to speak but she puts her finger over his lips. 'Don't answer that and stop frightening the natives.' She indicates with her head over her shoulder. 'I need the business.'

'Scouts honour.' Harry gives her the scouts salute (this time), she looks unconvinced but turns to leave him anyway. The couple have by now finished their meals so Rita stops to collect the empty plates.

'Empty plates, does that mean you enjoyed your meal?'

'One of the best all-day breakfasts we've had.' The man replies then beckons Rita to come closer, then in a hushed voice 'Is he safe? I mean would you prefer we stayed for a while?' Rita smiles.

'Harry's a pussy cat, I've known him forever, and he's probably more scared of me so don't worry. Can I get you anything else, a tea or coffee, on the house?'

'I'm fine.' The man's wife said.

'So am I thanks,' he lowers his voice again, 'if you're sure everything's ok we'll make a move.' Rita looks over at Harry who has now laid his head on his hands on the table.

'No worries, I'll look after him.' The couple smile then get up to leave. 'Thanks for coming and enjoy your stay.'

'We will,' answers the man who looks over towards Harry one more time, 'good luck.' he says as he nods his head in Harry's direction then leaves with his wife.

Sara pokes her head through the bamboo curtain.

'Have they gone?' She asks, 'and how's Harry?'

'Yes they have and Harry's pissed as a rat.'

'Oh dear,' Sara says as Rita passes her the empty plates then goes back into the kitchen. Rita turns back to the now sleeping Harry.

'Oh dear indeed,' Rita sighs to herself then goes to the coffee machine to make him a strong one, as she does this a group of girls come in.

'Are we too late for coffees?' one of them asks.

'Just coffee?'

'Any cakes?'

'Carrot cake.'

'Four cappuccinos and carrot cakes it is then.'

'Be with you in just a moment, take a seat, here.' Rita indicates the table nearest the counter as she finishes making Harry's coffee then looks into the kitchen. 'Sara, please could you sort out the cappuccinos and carrot cakes for these girls while I sort Harry out?'

'No problem Reet.' Rita takes the coffee over to Harry, the girls look over nervously in his direction.

'Is he all right Lady? He doesn't look very well.'

'He's fine, just had a bit too much to drink.' The girl looks as if she is about to stand up.

'Maybe we should go.'

'No worries girls,' Sara comes with the four cakes. 'He's an old friend of the family, here enjoy your cakes, coffees coming in a few minutes.' The girls look relieved and settle down to their cakes, Rita gives a half smile and mouths a thank you to Sara as she sits beside Harry.

'Harry,' she shakes him gently, 'come on wake up there's a nice hot, black coffee here for you.' Harry suddenly sits up and shakes his head which makes the girls jump, Rita waves reassuringly at them, they continue with their coffees with a smile.

'Are you in Brighton for long?' Sara asks the girls, Rita turns back to Harry.

'I'm fucked up Reet.'

'Language Harry there's some impressionable young ladies over there.' He looks over but they are talking and laughing now feeling relaxed.

'Mustn't frighten the customers eh?' Harry tries to give Rita a look to reassure her.

'How much did you have?'

'Barely anything.' They both laugh

'Well, can't drink as much as we used to, can we?'

'Not for the want of trying.'

'The boys don't seem to come down here as much.'

'No, it's not so easy for them, other than Ed I'm the only one who settled in Brighton.'

'How are they all?'

'Getting old, Steve thought he had prostate cancer, enjoyed telling us about the doc sticking his hand up his bum, but it seems he was clear.'

'He always was a bit of a hypochondriac, the others all right?'

'Ed wasn't there, he's in the Hove hospice with pancreatic cancer, seems he hasn't got long.' Rita pulls back in shock and sits down to compose herself.

'Oh no, that's awful, I wondered why he hadn't been in for a while, are you going to see him?'

'I want to, well, yes I am going, Steve was not very keen, and the other two said they'd go.'

'I can understand why Steve wouldn't want to go, they haven't spoken since he had the affair with Ed's wife.'

'Well he's hardly in a position to kill him like he threatened to.'

'No, he isn't,' Harry looks sad, 'Steve was always riding Ed's back, goading him, humiliating him, constantly poking fun, Ed was an easy target. The affair was the last straw, he forgave her of course, she was never really serious about Steve, and it was Ed's gambling that pushed her into his arms. I don't know why he ever hung around with us.'

'Because of the rest of you.'

'What were you doing on the beach anyway?' Rita asked to steer the conversation away from the subject of Ed's wife's infidelity.

'I don't really know, you'll probably think I'm a bloody idiot.'

'Look, I can be a bloody idiot as well.'

'You're no idiot.'

'So come on then, what was it?'

'I was remembering.'

'Good times or bad?'

'I was thinking about that first time we all came down here together, so a bit of both. So long ago now, I'm getting old.'

'You're not old, more like a vintage wine that improves with age.'

Harry laughs.

'Not so sure about the improving bit but thanks for the sentiment.' He swallows some coffee, Rita looks over to check on the girls who are finishing up.

'Just a minute, I forgot to get their money.' Harry nods whilst Rita goes over the girls, takes their cash, and exchanges a few comments until they get up to leave.

'Bye mate, hope you feel better soon.' One of them says to Harry as they pass by, he looks up and smiles.

'Thanks girls, sorry if I frightened you.'

'You didn't.' One of them answers, 'I don't think you could frighten anyone at the moment.' Then they giggle as they leave the café, Rita comes back to the table.

'How you getting home?'

'I think I've got enough for a taxi.'

'Save your money, come on I'll take you home,' she calls out to Sara, 'are you ok here while I take Harry home?'

'No problem Reet.'

'Thanks, ok come on then you old drunkard.'

'Yeah, in a minute, I've got to ask you something first.'

'Oh yes, what's that?' She asks as her eyes widen.

'Don't get too excited, I want you to come somewhere with me, do you think you might?'

'Tell me about it in the car.'

9.

Rita's ten year old Astra had more miles on the clock than Rita would have liked but it was a loyal workhorse and she didn't see the need to spend her retirement on a new one. Other than going back and forth from home to the café it didn't go really anywhere else except the cash and carry. It didn't take her long to make her way up to the Whitehawk area where Harry lived in a small two bedroomed house on the estate. They pull up outside, just along the road are a small group of boys, teenagers but school age, larking about around a car.

'Like it here do you?' Rita asks Harry.

'Not much but I don't really have a lot of choice do I?'

'Is it that bad?'

'Unless you like constant noise and swearing.'

'That bad eh? You could get out of Brighton all together. It's not the cheapest place in the country.'

'I could probably get an exchange but I've been here so long I'm not sure I could adjust to somewhere else. Then there are certain people I would miss.'

'Oh yes and who would they be?'

'As if you have to ask!'

'I can't imagine you'd really miss me.' Rita laughs.

'False modesty does not become you darling, you know I'd miss you.'

'Well come and see me more often.'

'I will, thanks for the lift, the food, the Alka-Seltzer and, well, thanks for everything actually.' Harry leans over and plants a light kiss on her cheek.'

'No problem, now go and sleep it off.'

'I will, and you don't mind about tomorrow?'

'Of course I don't, really.'

'You're one of the best Rita, one of the best, I....' Rita puts her finger on his lips.'

'Shhh, before you say something you'll regret.'

'I won't re.....'

'Shhh I said, now go home and sleep.'

'Bye Reet.'

'Bye Harry.' He steps out of the car and closes the door behind him. Rita smiles, waves and pulls away. Harry continues to wave to her until the car disappears around the corner.

'She your girlfriend grandad?' One of the youths calls out to him, 'giving 'er one are ya?' Harry turns to look at the group of boys narrowing his eyes at the one who spoke but says nothing. There are five of them, he slowly looks at from one to the other. 'What are you looking at you old peado, want to shag one of us do ya? Go on fuck off.'

Harry smiles, shakes his head, walks up to his door and lets himself in whilst the boy continues to jeer at him. He looks back once more to notice one of them isn't laughing but looks away when Harry tries to lock eyes. After another few seconds Harry turns away, goes inside, closes the door and leans back against it with a sigh.

'Don't rise to the bait Harry boy, don't let the little shits get to you, it won't end well.' He walks through to the kitchen without turning the lights on, opens the fridge, where there is nothing much. A tub of margarine, a bottle of milk, a small lump of cheese and a solitary can of draught Guinness which he extracts and opens. He waits the few seconds it takes the widget to fizz and looks around for a clean glass but the sink is full of dirty ones. He takes a swig from the can, rinses out a glass and pours the rest into it.

Harry goes to the window, closes the curtains then sits down to turn on the TV. The room is a mess, dirty plates on the table with a number of empty beer cans littering it as well as the floor.

'I really should tidy this place up,' he looks around at the mess, he hadn't noticed how bad it was getting, after a while the brain doesn't register anymore. His eyes fall to the photographs on his cupboard, he stands up and goes over to them. Smiling he picks up one with the younger Harry sitting on his Lambretta. A feeling of sadness washes over him as he stares at the innocent boy looking confident all those years ago.

'What went wrong Harry boy, where did that boy who was going to rock the world with his band go?' He puts the photograph down again. 'He gave up that's what he did, let a woman get in the way of his ambition, and they don't mix with the music, do they?'

He reaches out to touch the photograph once more, stirring memories he thought he had buried deep. With that Harry goes through the kitchen to the door that led him into the garage. He groped in the dark for the pull string to turn on the light which wasn't that bright.

Inside there are piles of boxes making it look like a warehouse storing ancient artefacts, some of which actually are. There was a shelf with a few hundred vinyl albums, all the good stuff, Small Faces, The Who, The Stones, Beatles, Kinks, Jam, Secret Affair and many more. Worth a lot of money now but no matter how desperate he might get for cash he would never sell them, even if he didn't have anything to play them on.

He pulls out the Who's original version of Quadrophenia, a double album. It cost him and arm and a leg back in 1978 but it was worth every penny. Housed in the centre of the fold out sleeve was a book containing all the lyrics and many photographs following the story. With nostalgia washing over him Harry slowly looked through it, softly singing the words to '5.15' as he did so.

'Out of my brain on the five, fifteen!' he sings the chorus line loudly and smiles, 'I really have to dig out the CD, haven't heard it for a while.' He says to himself then carefully replaces the album on the shelf. All his vinyl albums are in near mint condition, he would never lend or borrow records as they were too personal to whoever owned them. He would have hated to damage someone else's vinyl and knew others wouldn't treat his with the same care he would. It caused a few arguments at the time but if they didn't understand his point of view it was their problem, not his.

He had a lot of albums by The Who, despite really liking Quadrophenia 'Who's Next' was his favourite with the tracks 'Won't Get Fooled Again' and especially 'Behind Blue Eyes.' He thought maybe he'd play that instead when he got back inside the house. It had been some time since he'd looked at his collection, thumbing along the spines he stopped at the Small Faces album 'Ogden's Nut Gone Flake' with the round fold out cover, another collectable item. He doesn't pull it out, just runs his hand along the spines once more and turns away.

There was a box of old video tapes as well and he did still have an old VHS machine that when the mood took him he'd watch Quadrophenia or Tommy on it but he didn't feel like right now. In one corner was a box of rolled up posters, from a lot of the gigs he'd been to, The Jam, Selector, Secret Affair, Merton Parkas and a host of other would be Mod bands who didn't make it and whose names were long forgotten - a bit like himself he thought. They would be worth money as well, especially the signed Jam poster.

It had been the Hammersmith Odeon, as it was called then, now it's the Apollo. Harry, Steve and Ed had queued for what seemed like hours to get tickets. The seats hadn't been great, near the back but that meant they could get out quickly when the band played the last encore. Harry had managed to get a poster out of one of the displays so the three of them hoofed it round to the stage door to catch the band making their exit whilst the crowd were still crying for more. Bruce and Rick had been friendly enough and signed with no problem, Paul Weller on the other hand had to be shamed by the other two into putting his name on it.

They missed the last train to Catford and it was a long walk back home. His mother read the riot act when he finally made it, of course he hadn't thought to phone to explain. She said she would have paid for a taxi, 'Hadn't thought of that' he said.

The poster made it home in one piece, Harry treasured it and had been meaning to get it framed one day, even if it was now a little frayed around the edges. He ran his fingers along the spines of the albums then took the poster out of the tube to look at it once more, smiling at the memory of the night he met The Jam.

Finally his eyes rested on what sat in the centre of the floor, a tarpaulin covered item with a thick layer of dust that filled the air and his nostrils as he shook it off. With a crash the tarpaulin falls to the floor to reveal his once pride and joy, a Lambretta. It had been many moons since Harry had uncovered the old machine and even longer since he'd ridden it. Lovingly Harry runs his hand over the handlebars and the body, he'd removed some of the badges years ago but he knew they were in a box, somewhere.

It wasn't taxed or insured but probably had half a gallon or so of petrol in the tank. To check he pulled the seat up to reveal the tank and opened the cap to see if he was correct in his assumption.

'I wonder if it'll start.' He muttered to himself as he lifted his leg over to the kick starter and tried three times to turn the engine over but then realised the battery was flat. 'Now where's that charger?' he asked himself and starts to search the garage having some idea where it might be. After moving some boxes of tools he hits the jackpot.

'OK let's get you charged up.' With that he connected the clips to the terminals without removing the battery from the machine and plugged it into the mains. 'Tomorrow we'll have a look to see what it takes to get you on the road again, just like old times my lovely, just like old times.'

10.

Meanwhile on the other side of town Terry Weismann, pronounced Vice-man was tuning a Yamaha XVS1300 Custom he had just sold to one of his best customers. Ten grand plus worth of chopper style bike with a 1300CC engine that could leave most things behind. Whilst preparing it for the road, (the customer would be picking it up in the morning,) he wished he could afford one himself. He was however realistic that at his age, unless he won the lottery of course, there was very little chance of that happening. It was some awesome machine. Still, his old Triumph Bonneville, which he'd had for more years than he could think of, was still a cool runner. He loved that machine, more than his girlfriend, as she would constantly tell him.

His father, Jürgen, had been a German prisoner of war, captured in Normandy just after D.Day. Like many of his countrymen of the time he was mesmerised by Adolf Hitler and joined the Hitler Youth before the war. He eventually joined the army when he was seventeen, by which time the war in the east was all but lost, with the Russians pushing the German forces back to the fatherland. Jürgen was sent to France to defend against the anticipated invasion by the allies.

After he was captured, along with thousands of other prisoners was taken to England and eventually Normanhurst Camp near Battle in Sussex. As the war drew to a close he spent his days working on a nearby farm. Here the teenage Jürgen met young Linda Thomas who was working as a land girl on the same farm. In no time they fell in love. When the war was over he was due to be repatriated to his home land but when he found that his entire family had been killed in the raid on Dresden, Jürgen opted to stay in England.

Linda's father was against her marrying 'a bloody Nazi' so they had to wait until she turned twenty one in 1947. The mother however had been supportive. Jürgen had quickly learnt English whilst he was working on the farm, which he continued to do while studying to be a motor mechanic. He had no problem finding employment, having taken to engines like a duck to water.

Mr Thomas eventually accepted his son in law, realising he wasn't the 'bloody Nazi' he had thought he was, and helped him to open his own garage in the sixties, Terry was born in 1954 and his sister a year later. Fascinated by the skill his father had handling spanners he quickly learnt to do the same, by the time he was fifteen he could strip an engine and put it back together with ease.

Jürgen developed a passion for motorcycle racing and would often take Terry to see races at Brands Hatch which is how his son developed his love for motorbikes and the sport, as well as rock and roll music. Terry did however spend some time in prison when he was twenty one, he wasn't proud of what he did and had been on the straight and narrow ever since. Jürgen died in 1993 leaving Terry to take over the garage which he continued to run to this day.

Elvis Presley's greatest hits were playing on the workshop's CD player with Terry singing along to every track. He was looking forward to maybe passing the business on to his grandson, his daughter's only child. He was still a bit young at fifteen and didn't really seem to have any interest in the trade despite his grandfather's efforts to stir one.

It was all starting to get a bit too much for Terry to cope with, even with the two staff he had, who seemed to change constantly. Retirement age was still a few years away; sure he could retire when he wanted to but the pension wouldn't be as much. Not only that, he didn't know what to do about the workshop. It had been his father's, back in the day and he had hoped to have a son to take over, but only a daughter.

Terry was long since divorced, his daughter Julia had been a teenager at the time opting to live with her father whilst her mother went off to America with a new husband. He now lived with a long term girlfriend, a few years younger than him, who had no children of her own.

Time was marching on, the workshop should have closed half an hour before but he was determined to have the bike ready before going home, just in case the customer came in early the next day. At the moment he was satisfied, about to clean the oil and grease from his hands, the phone rang. He wanted to ignore it, after all he was supposed to be closed, but couldn't for long, never could.

'Weismann's, be quick I'm closing up soon.' A voice spoke to him on the other end of the line. 'OK Jimmy, let me know when you're going and I'll come with you.'

The line went dead, Terry held the receiver for a few seconds longer before replacing it in the cradle, his mood had changed and the news had not been good.

11.

Harry woke up on his sofa, Good Morning Britain was silently playing on the TV. He couldn't remember what he'd been watching the night before after coming back into the house from the garage. He did remember having a few whiskies, well more than a few as his pounding head testified to. With a groan he prised himself up to stagger into the kitchen in search of medicinal relief which he found in a draw by the cooker. After swallowing more than the recommended dose he put on the kettle to make a very strong cup of coffee.

'That's the last time I drink that much booze.' He declared to no one in particular and laughed at the comment. 'Now how many times have I said that over the year? I shouldn't anyway, not with the anti-biotics.'

He then goes back to the same drawer to find a packet of stale cigarettes stuffed in the back. 'And of course I've given up smoking, haven't I Rita? Just one more.'

There is only one in the packet, which Harry takes out and rolls around in his fingers, equally wanting so much to smoke and not smoke it. He puts it down on the kitchen worktop while making himself the coffee that he sips carefully because it is so hot. Picking up the cigarette once more he takes it, with the coffee, upstairs to the bedroom where he strips off his clothes preparing to take a shower.

A sudden nausea overtakes him so he rushes to the bathroom and barely makes it to the toilet before emptying his stomach of whatever was in there. Most of it was liquid, being as how he'd hardly eaten anything the night before. It was also very dark due to the copious amount of Guinness he'd drunk.

'Ohhh that's better.' He sighs whilst standing up, reaching for some toilet paper to wipe his mouth clean and genuinely feeling much improved. Harry returned to the coffee for another sip but the taste of vomit still present in this mouth discouraged him from lighting the cigarette, the urge had subsided.

With that he stepped in to the shower.

Harry let the water cascade over him for quite some time, gradually washing away the hangover, but not completely. When he finally emerged from the bathroom Harry put on his dressing gown to go back to the kitchen for more coffee. He was now feeling extremely hungry but all there was to eat was some stale bread and a jar of ginger marmalade.

'Better than nothing I suppose.' He said to himself as he feeds two slices into the toaster and refills the kettle. As soon as he takes a bite from the first slice, the telephone rang so he quickly swallowed the mouthful and grabbed it to press the answer button.

'Hello, if you're trying to sell me something or going on about PPI you can fu….'

'Harry,' Rita interrupted him 'no I'm not trying to sell you anything, just wanted to see how you are this morning, I thought I'd waiting long enough for you to have thrown up and showered.'

'You know me so well, the head's improving, I'm on my second coffee and yes I've done both.' Rita laughs.

'So as to what you asked me on the way home last night, of course I'll come with you, is tomorrow morning ok? Sara can open the café for me, I'll pick you up at ten.'

'Fab, I'll see you then.' With a smile Harry hangs up the phone. 'I have work to do today.'

After finishing his coffee and toast Harry puts on some old clothes, picks up his portable CD player from the kitchen and takes it with a handful of discs into the garage.

'Now where shall we start?' He says to himself whilst setting up the CD player, 'let's have The Who first, bit of Who's Next.' With the disc in the player Harry hits the play button, turns up the volume really loud and the strains of 'Baba O'Reilly' fill the garage.

Whilst singing along with the CD, Harry proceeds to strip the bike down, first removing the panels before taking the engine apart. He hadn't done this for many years but he could do it with ease, even with his eyes closed. Working through the day the music moved on from The Who through The Jam, The Chords and all the tunes from his younger years, music he hadn't really heard for quite a while.

He lost track of time until, eventually, his stomach knocked loudly reminding him that he hadn't eaten since the two slices of stale toast some hours ago. Realising there was nothing to eat in the house he calls for a pizza delivery which, he ravenously devours, with heavily oil stained hands, when it arrives.

With all the parts stripped and laid out carefully Harry sits down in the old chair he keeps in the garage and promptly falls asleep, exhausted.

After sleeping for almost two hours he wakes up feeling stiff and aching in all his limbs to survey all the work he has done on the bike. More than satisfied he leaves everything as it is with the intention of returning after meeting with Rita in the morning.

'I'll have you back in tip top condition in no time old girl, just you wait and see. I just don't know if I can afford to get you back on the road.'

12.

The weather was still somewhat overcast and getting darker by the minute, not that unusual for the time of year but when you know any day soon will be your last you kind of want the sun to shine. Which is exactly how Edward (Ed) Rawlings felt when he woke up this morning in the hospice where he had been for the past week. His intravenous drip of morphine that he referred to as 'the bomb', clicked to indicate a fresh dose had been pumped into his system. It helped but he could still feel the pain, albeit not as bad as it would be without it. He could override the timer if he really needed to and would regularly do so, the buzz was good and what was it going to do, kill him? So he clicked it twice, now that was better.

Ed had been born in Lewisham hospital, the second son to his proud parents, he would be followed by two sisters.

He fell in love with Brighton when he first ventured down with Harry, Steve and Bernie back in the late seventies. Okay the first time had not gone so well but they came back again and again, mainly because of Harry, who had found love. It didn't take Ed long to find it either and not just the town, there had been Sheila had been older than him, a lot older but that hadn't bothered Ed as she was the love of his life and had given him a wonderful daughter in Denise. Sure she'd once had a brief affair with Steve, he couldn't really blame her. Ed's gambling addiction had lost them their house. Steve had come to visit, not knowing the situation, Ed was elsewhere and Sheila burst into tears and poured her heart out to him. One thing led to another and they ended up in bed together. They only met a handful of times after that until Sheila couldn't deal with the guilt anymore and told Ed everything.

Ed forgave her but at first he had wanted to kill Steve as it seemed to be the final straw from someone who had always given him a hard time. He seriously considered it, Sheila however, managed to calm him down and it would be a few years before Ed saw Steve again. It would be Harry's instigation of the annual reunion that brought them together again. He might have forgiven his wife but would never forgive Steve whose betrayal cut deeper than her's.

When Sheila died of kidney failure a year ago it was the end of his world, if it hadn't been for Denise and his grandson Sammy, he wasn't sure if he could have carried on. However, carry on he did until the pains started, at first his local GP couldn't find anything wrong. An X-Ray didn't reveal anything so he sent him for a scan, by which time the pain had become excruciating and his skin a shade of yellow. As soon as the consultant in the hospital took one look at Ed's face he admitted him immediately.

After a hasty scan the diagnosis had not been good, it was pancreatic cancer and too far advanced to operate. The doctor gave him weeks rather than months, so within a few days Ed was transferred to the hospice in Hove where he now waited for the inevitable.

It was early, Ed looked over to the weather station clock on his bedside cabinet. The time was 06.20, the temperature a constant 24 degrees, the rest of the display Ed just didn't understand, nor did he care. Despite the fact he wasn't really eating solids he could feel a need to shit as well as an urge to piss. Dignity, what was that? Not something someone dying of pancreatic cancer had the privilege of having. Not being sure if he could wait for a nurse to come and help with this urgent call of nature, Ed pressed his call button.

Nurse Petra Kaminski, a pretty young twenty something, born in England from Polish immigrants came as soon as she could. Ed liked her and she seemed to like him, he just didn't like having to do his thing with her assisting, not a lot of choice there.

'Good morning Mr Rawlings, how are you feeling today?'

'I'd feel a lot better if you called me Ed.'

'All right, Ed, how are you feeling today?'

'I've pumped a couple of extra tots of morph into me this morning so I'm kind of floating on clouds a little bit, is that a bad thing?'

Nurse Kaminski leant in close to Ed's ear.

'If it makes you feel good, do it, but don't tell anyone I said so.' Ed laughed. 'Will your daughter come in today?' She asked.

'I'm sure she will, she's a good girl, been a rock ever since her mother died, I don't know how I would have coped otherwise.'

Petra knew what Ed wanted without asking and proceeded to deal with it in a matter of fact way making him feel at ease, chatting at the same time.

'Do you only have the one daughter, no sons?'

'No, just Denise, my wife was forty two when she was born, bit late in life and unexpected, she was a bit older than me. What about you, married, children?'

'Oh no, not me, well, not for a while anyway, I'm only twenty five with no ambitions for either at the moment.'

'Boyfriend………….. Girlfriend?' Petra laughs.

'I've got a boyfriend but nothing serious, he's certainly not 'the one' but fun to have around for the time being.'

'What's his name?'

'Roy.'

'What does he do?'

'He's a policeman.'

'Good job, is he good to you?'

'Yeah, he is.'

'But you're looking for something better?'

'I wouldn't say something better, I'm just not sure I love him like I should do to commit long term. How did you know you're wife was the one?'

'People talk about that magical moment when you know someone is 'the one' but I think it's something you grow into. If it feels good at the start, go for it, when you start to miss them after a short time apart then maybe, just maybe they are getting to be more important to you. When did you last see Roy?'

'Sunday.'

'What day is it today?'

'Tuesday.'

'So do you miss him?' Petra considers the question for a few moments.

'I guess so.'

'And is the sex good?' She laughs and softly playfully punches Ed on the arm.

'Ed, what are you like?'

'Seriously, is it good?'

'Yeah, it's pretty damn good.'

'Maybe you like him more than you think you do then.' She stands back, folds her arms and narrows her eyes at Ed.

43

'Mr Rawlings, maybe you know me better than I know myself, you've got me thinking.'

'Good!'

'Now, can I do anything else for you as I have to get on with my duties?'

'No I'm fine thanks but maybe you could bring Roy in to visit me sometime soon, I have a busy schedule you know and I wouldn't want to miss him.' Petra smiled.

'Yes, I'll do that, maybe tomorrow.'

'I'll have my secretary check my diary but I'm sure tomorrow will be fine.'

They both laugh, Petra touches Ed's hand affectionately and leaves the room. Ed smiles and thinks back to the day he met Sheila. He had been visiting Brighton for a number of years since that first trip with Harry and the gang. Many of them had been with his friends but this time he caught the train and came alone. The intention had been to just do what he pleased without Steve controlling everything they, and especially Ed, did. Steve was a bit of a control freak and Ed didn't really understand why they were friends. Steve could be fun to be with at times, this time however, Ed didn't want to be controlled he just wanted to explore what Brighton had to offer, alone.

Just off the train he made his way to The Lanes, there was a second hand record shop there and armed with a few quid his intention was to pick up some bargains. He was on a mission, striding forcefully towards his destination when he crashed into a woman coming around a corner sending her flying to the ground.

'I…….I'm so sorry.' Ed stuttered as he leant down to help her back to her feet. 'Are you okay?'

'A little shaken but I'll live.' She rubbed her arm where there was a minor graze then bent to pick up her bag, Ed moved to do the same and their heads cracked together.'

'I'm so sorry, again.' They both rubbed their heads and started to laugh, the woman picked up her bag with the tell-tale sound of broken glass. 'Ah that didn't sound good, what was it?'

The woman looked inside her bag and sighed.

'Not important, a small vase I just bought, it didn't cost much.'

'I'm so sorry, again.'

'Like I said not important, I can get another one.'

'How much was it? I'll give you the money.'

'No worries, it was as much my fault, I wasn't looking where I was going either.'

'No really, I have to give you something.'

'Honestly, it was a couple of quid in a charity shop, forget it.'

'Maybe, maybe I can buy you a drink as compensation.' She looked at her watch then back at Ed.

'Well, all right, just a quick one, I have to get back to work, what's your name?'

'Ed, my name's Ed.'

'Pleased to meet you Ed, I'm Sheila.'

'Mr Rawlings, how are you today?' The voice of the doctor brought Ed out of his reminiscing.

'Much the same as yesterday only the pain is getting worse, hence my upping the dose of my meds.'

'Try not to do that too much.'

'Why, will it kill me?' Ed laughs but the doctor looks disapprovingly at him.

'Maybe a bit sooner rather than later.'

'I'll risk it.'

'Hmph!' was all the doctor could say, 'I'll be seeing you Mister Rawlings.'

'Have a nice day doc.' Ed murmured but the doctor had already left the room so Ed closed his eyes and carried on thinking about the day he met Sheila.

She led him to a nearby pub, the woman behind the bar knew *Sheila* and winked at her when Ed bought the drinks. Ed saw the wink but chose to pretend that he hadn't.

At the time he was twenty three and realised she was older but wouldn't ask her age, guessing it was the wrong side of thirty. After the second drink and non-stop conversation he knew that he was in love and wanted to be with her forever. She wasn't married but had a long term boyfriend, Ed was crestfallen when she told him.

This didn't stop them exchanging telephone numbers.

Ed had only been home a day when she called him, asking if he would be coming back to Brighton anytime soon. He had decided he wouldn't call her, with a boyfriend on the scene Ed considered it pointless. However, here she was calling him, wanting to see him again.

So that weekend Ed caught the train to Brighton once more where *Sheila* met him. To his surprise she threw her arms around his neck and kissed him, hard, tongues and all, he didn't resist.

'I'm thirty five, is that a problem for you?'

'Oh no,' Ed replied, 'no problem at all.'

He was still smiling at the memory when he drifted back to sleep.

13.

Ed woke with a start when he felt someone touching his hand.

'What the!?' He looked around the room at some very familiar faces.

'Hello you old bugger.' Rita leant in to kiss him on the forehead as his eyes started to focus on her, Harry, Steve, Frank and Bernie.

'I thought I might escape this life without having to see you lot again.'

'Oh don't be like that Ed.' Rita said with a pout 'what have I done to you?'

'Not you Rita, you've always been kind to me, unlike some of these I could mention.'

'I suppose you mean me.' Steve chipped in.

'If the cap fits…..' Ed replied.

'Oh come on, I'm here aren't I, doesn't that count for something?'

'Yeah Steve, you're here and yes it does.' Steve nods and bites his lip, forcing back tears that he doesn't realise he was about to shed.

'Why didn't you say anything mate?' Harry asked.

'It all happened so quickly.'

'You seemed all right at Denise's wedding.' Bernie said.

'I had quite a bit of pain then but I didn't know it was so serious, at least I got to see her married.'

'I thought you looked out of salts.' Frank added

Harry puts his hand out to touch him on the shoulder, Ed looks at it knowingly.

'What have you been working on, looks like oil and grease on your hands?' Ed asks.

'You're still sharp then.' Harry replies

'You've been working on the old girl haven't you?' Harry laughs. 'You sly old bastard - going to ride her again?'

'That's the plan.' Rita shoots him a look, Harry avoids her eyes.

'Just like old times eh?' Ed says.

'Yeah just like old times.' Harry replies and the pair of them start to laugh, which obviously causes Ed some pain.

'You still got it?' Steve asks.

'Of course, haven't you?'

'Well, yes I have.' Steve replies.

'Me too.' Says Bernie.

'And me.' Frank adds. They all laugh together.

'Wish I could see them all.' Says Ed, 'and ride with you all one last time.'

'Maybe you will.' Harry says.

'Sadly, not in this life mate.' With that the room goes quiet with them all understanding the implications of what Ed said.

'Do you want to bet on that?' Steve asks with his tongue firmly planted in his cheek.

'Gave all that up a long time ago,' Ed laughs, 'just not long enough ago.'

'How's the pain mate, if you don't mind me asking?' Bernie asks him.

'Bad, well it would be really bad if it wasn't for this thing here.' With that he picks up his bomb. 'Pumps morphine in on a regular basis, plus I can click this button and get and extra dose if I want it.' As if to demonstrate Ed does just that and laughs.

'Blimey, drugs on tap.' Bernie laughs 'at least there is an upside to cancer.'

'Yeah but one I'd rather not have.' Ed says through his laugh.

'I've stripped the old girl down,' Harry says, changing the subject to try and lighten the mood. 'Trouble is after all this time I'm not sure if I need to replace any parts.'

'Rita,' Ed turns towards her, 'there's a notepad and pen in my locker there, perhaps you could fish them out for me, please?'

'Yes, sure.' Rita opens up the locker where she finds the items he asked for and passes them to Ed who proceeds to write something, the gang look at each other lifting eyelids questioningly.

'What are you doing?' Frank asks.

'Writing a shopping list, gimme a minute will ya!' Ed continues to write, when he finishes he folds the paper and writes something else then hands it to Harry. 'This is my daughter's address, go and see her and my son in law, he's a good bloke, and give this to them.'

Harry opens it up and reads it.

'Ed I can't....'

'It's the least I can do, you're a good friend, and besides, what can I do with it from here?'

'You're a good mate Ed.'

'So are you, all of you, even Steve.' He reaches out for Steve's hand.

'I thought you hated me.' Steve mumbled, 'I mean I always gave you such a hard time and there was............' he trails off knowing Ed understood what he was going to say.

'Yeah you got on my tits most of the time, but you always had my, sorry, our backs so no, I don't hate you............... and I've forgiven you.'

He didn't have to say for what.

'Had some good times though didn't we?' Bernie asked.

'Of course we did and I treasure them, now fuck off all of you I'm feeling really tired.' They all laugh.

'We'll be back again soon.' Frank ascertains.

'You'd better.' Ed responds, 'I'm going nuts in here fighting off the nurses.' The gang wave and file out of the room with Steve last out the door, he stops and turns back to face Ed.

'I'm going to miss you dude.' He says quietly.

''I'm gonna miss you too.' Ed smiles one last time as Steve waves again and turns away.

14.

'Group Hug!' Steve whispers to them all as they stand in the car park of the Hospice, with a solemn look on their faces they all throw their arms around each other. After what seemed like an hour but was in fact less than half a minute they moved apart. Rita had tears in her eyes while the boys were obviously fighting them back.

'So he'll be with Sheila soon.' Rita sounded hopeful.

'I wish I could believe that,' Harry replied, 'but you know that I don't'

'Neither do I,' Steve added.

'Or me,' sighed Frank.

'The Jury is out on that one as far as I'm concerned, can't say he will or he won't, I'd like to believe he will, especially for Ed's sake.' Bernie said as he reached out to touch Rita affectionately on her hand.

'I don't think he's got much longer,' Harry states, 'They don't move you into a hospice for a long term stay, I'd say he's got a week, maybe ten days and he'll go downhill pretty quick as they up the morphine, so we should come back in a couple of days, everyone agree?'

Everyone nods in agreement, Steve however doesn't look so sure.

'Steve?' Frank looks at him, 'problem?'

'Ah no, no problem, same time day after tomorrow.' Everyone nods in agreement, shake hands and disperse to their cars. Harry with Rita, while the others travelled together in Steve's car. Harry and Rita wave to them as they pull out of the car park.

'Come on, I'll take you home.' Rita loops her arm through Harry's and steers him back to her car.

'We're all getting to that age aren't we?'

'What age is that?' Rita asks as she opens the car doors for them to get in.

'The age where we start going to funerals, eventually our own.'

'Come on don't be such a depressive, you're only sixty, don't you know it's the new fifty?'

'Yeah, but Ed, he won't see sixty.' Rita leans over to take his hand for comfort.

'That doesn't mean anything is going to happen to you.'

'Doesn't it?'

'Come on love, let me get you home.' She grips his hand once more, starts the engine and pulls away. It was only a short drive through the town back to Harry's house. They drove in silence, both of them in their thoughts about Ed, what he had lost and what he was about to lose.

Back at the house the gang of youths were once again hanging around nearby. Rita looked over at them nervously.

'Do you want me to stay for a bit?'

'No I'll be all right, you get back to Sara, she's probably swamped with orders for coffee and cake.' Rita laughs.

'I should be so lucky at this time of the year.'

'You never know,' he leans over to kiss her on the cheek.

'Don't be a stranger.'

'Never.'

'The coffee machine is always on and there's plenty of bacon in the fridge.'

'How can I refuse such an offer?' He gives her one more peck on the cheek, gets out of the car and watches her drive away around the corner out of sight. Turning towards his house he could hear shouting and glass breaking.

'Don't get involved,' Harry says to himself whilst putting the key in the lock. The crying coming from the distant alleyway sounded desperate, he sighed and removed the key from the lock. Striding forcefully he turns into the alleyway in just a few short seconds. There he sees the same gang of boys that were goading him recently. They were kicking several bags of shit out of another lad who was lying on the ground, desperately trying to protect his head from the boots. One of the aggressors spots Harry and points him out to the others who stop and turn his way.

Harry recognises one of them as the youth who had mouthed off to him a few days before. With a smile on his face the teenager immediately continued to do so.

'What are you looking at, you old prick?' Harry doesn't respond, just leans against the wall of the alley and focuses his attention on the body groaning on the ground.

'Maybe he's deaf.' One of the others comments making the rest of them laugh.

'Yeah, I've heard old queers like it up the arse and any other hole as well.' The head youth added. 'Do you like it up the arse you old perv? Can you hear me?' He raises his voice to a shout. 'Getting a bit deaf in your old age are you?'

'I can hear you just fine.' Harry replies in a calm voice without raising it. 'I could hear your stupid voice half a block away.'

'You what?' The boy starts to march up to Harry who doesn't move from his place against the wall

'Now it's you that seems to be going deaf, I SAID!' Harry starts to shout, 'I could hear your stupid voice half a block away.'

'Why don't you piss off back to your care home you old cunt, before I break your face?' Harry chuckles.

'I'd like to see you try.'

'Don't tempt me old man, don't you know who I am?'

'No, should I?'

'Yeah, I'm the leader around here.'

Harry bursts out laughing.

'Leader? What of, the Kindergarten?'

'If you don't know now you soon will.'

'No, I don't know, or care that much either.'

'What?'

'Do you know who I am?'

'No, don't ca...'

'That's my point.' Harry cuts him off nonchalantly waving his hand at nothing in particular. The youth looks unsure of what to do, the other boys slowly edge their way towards them. Harry doesn't take his eyes off the youth. 'You don't know who or what I am, you think your bravado and this gang of cronies are enough to frighten people.' Still waving his hand and leaning on the wall Harry burns his eyes into the youth's who is starting to look uncertain. He pushes himself away from the wall, pulling up to his full height. This sees him towering over the boy who steps back slightly, not much but enough to show how uncertain he is.

'You think everyone is scared of you, don't you? It's probably how you manage to keep this bunch of monkeys in line. You should be careful who you pick on, I mean, could you take on that poor guy on your own? What did he do to you to deserve that beating?' The boy opens his mouth to speak but Harry cuts him off. 'I don't care what he did, I just hate bullies and you sonny, are a bully.'

Harry pokes him in the chest.

'You can't do that to me.'

'Can't I? You see, I'm not scared of you, or your mates, I've had bigger than you for breakfast, dinner and tea. But you, you're scared aren't you? Not had someone stand up to you before, am I right?'

The boy doesn't answer.

'No? Well you have now, so, what are you going to do about it?'

Harry leans in close to the boy, so close he could feel the teenager's breath on his face.

'You're terrified aren't you?' He leans in close to his ear and whispers, 'just a terrified child, have you wet yourself?' The boy steps back.

'I'll show you terrified.' He answers in a shaky voice and takes a swing at Harry who deftly side steps, leaving the boy's fist making contact with thin air, and losing his balance. Harry punches him squarely on the jaw sending him back into his mates who catch and quickly stand him upright. They start to laugh at him until he turns back with a look that could kill. Turning back to Harry he digs into his pocket and brings out a flick knife that locks into place in flash. The boys move back from him, Harry stands his ground as the boy waves the knife in his face.

'Who's terrified now old man?'

'Well, you by the looks of things, if you really thought you could take me, you wouldn't need that.'

'I'm going to cut you paedo.'

'You should think about what you're doing here laddie, before you make a huge mistake.'

'I have thought about it and I want to cut you, real bad.' He makes a few short jabbing movements towards Harry who doesn't bat an eyelid.

'Won't be the first time laddie.'

The boy lunges forward, but once more Harry side steps and punches him in the side of the head. His mates are getting nervous and shout out for him to stop and put the knife away but he doesn't listen.

'You can all fuck off if you're too yellow to fight him, I'm going to make him so sorry he tangled with me.'

'Last chance boy, I don't want to really hurt you.'

'As if old man, as if.' He charges towards Harry and slashes the knife through the air but Harry is faster and grips the boy's wrist. Just as swiftly he brings his right foot down on the back of the boy's knee forcing him to the ground on his knees like a sack of potatoes. He screams as Harry twists his wrist making him drop the knife that clatters to the ground. While still holding the boy's wrist Harry puts a foot on his chest pushing him to the ground then leans down to pick up the knife.

'Now this is an important lesson, just because you think someone looks easy to beat, some old geezer like me for instance, doesn't mean that you can. Sure you could hope your boys here would jump in to back you up but I'd snap your neck first.'

'You fucking old cunt, I'll have you yet.'

'Maybe, maybe not, or maybe I'll have you first, anyway I'll be keeping the knife. Did you know it was illegal to carry a flick knife? At the moment you're just looking at an assault charge.'

'I didn't assault you, you attacked me!' The boy struggles to his feet.

'After you took a swing at me, that's self-defence and what about chummy over there, what do you call his cuts and bruises? No you're just looking at an assault charge, should I choose to take you down the Old Bill station. However, the knife, well that puts a different slant on things, possession of deadly weapon................. attempted murder even. What do you think, shall I go and tell the cops you tried to stab me? I've got at least one witness who will testify.'

The boy looks uncertain.

'I know most of the coppers down at Brighton nick, very well indeed, so who do you think they are likely to believe? Me? Or a miserable scrote like you?

'I was just,' he starts to stutter, 'just trying to scare you, that's all.'

'That went well then didn't it? Now, I don't know you but I do know you wouldn't last five minutes in jail, you'd be someone's bitch in no time, if you're not eaten alive first. Or you could just fuck off and never come back, what's it gonna be, cop station or the off?'

'I live around here.'

'Should have thought about that first.'

'Fuck off, I've got nowhere to go.'

'So the Old Bill it is.' Harry reaches out to grab his arm, the boy tries to wriggle free but Harry's grip is too tight. 'What's your name boy?'

'Pete, my name's Pete.' His friends start to back away a bit further whilst the boy they had been beating (on) stands up and leans against the wall whilst wiping the blood away from his mouth and nose with his handkerchief.

'We'll see you around Pete.' One of them calls out as they turn away to make a hasty retreat around the corner and out of sight.

'Can't trust anyone these days can you Pete?' Pete is starting to look really scared, Harry looks over at the wounded boy. 'Who are you son?'

'Charlie.'

'Charlie what?'

'Does it matter?'

'I like to know who I'm fighting for.'

'Charlie Conrad.'

'Pleased to meet you Charlie Conrad, I'm Harry York.'

'Really pleased to meet you Harry York.'

'Are you OK?'

'Might have a broken rib or two, head's not feeling to good either but I think I'll live.'

'Good, good so only ABH for you and attempted murder on me, ready to go see the Old Bill Pete?'

'Look mister, Harry...............'

'NO! YOU LOOK PETEY!' Harry sighs and grabs the boy's other arm to look him squarely in the eyes. 'Okay, you live near here, I can be magnanimous, go home, but I better not see you in this street again or I will take you and this knife, with your fingerprints on to talk to my good friend Sergeant Lewis at Brighton police station. Deal?'

'Deal.' Pete agrees reluctantly, Harry lets go of his arm.

'Wise choice Pete, very wise choice.' Pete backs quickly away from Harry.

'This isn't over old man.' He shouts back at Harry.

'Oh it had better be Sonny Jim, you really don't want to go to war with me, now fuck off before I change my mind.'

'It's not over!' With that Pete spits on the floor, flips a V sign and stalks off angrily.

'Oh, it never is.' Harry whispers to himself, 'it never is.'

'He's a head case Harry.' Charlie tells him.

'Some friends you've got.'

'What's it to you anyway?'

'I've just saved your arse, that's what it's got to do with me.'

'Yeah, well,' Charlie avoids Harry's gaze, 'thanks for that.'

'That wasn't so bad was it?'

'I suppose, but I could have handled him if it hadn't been for the others.'

'Really? Looks like they were handling you.'

'I know how to fight, my dad taught me,' Harry smiles.

'Pity, you shouldn't have to, where do you live?'

'Couple of street away, Ramsey Street.'

'Well you need to get back there, you're mum will be getting worried.'

'She's not around, only Dad.'

'Well he'll be wondering where you are,' Charlie shuffles his feet, Harry shrugs his shoulders.

'I don't want to go home yet.'

'Well maybe you're right there, I should get you cleaned up a bit before you do, come on.'

Harry turns to make his way home, Charlie doesn't move at first.

'Well are you coming or not?'

After a few seconds follows him out of the alley.

Back at Harry's house he cleans Charlie's cuts and applies some antiseptic cream to them.

'There's nothing I can do for your ribs, pull your shirt up and let me see.' Charlie obeys and Harry tenderly touches them where bruises are already starting to show.

'Ouch! That hurts!' Charlie cries out.

'Sorry, but I don't think they are cracked or broken just badly bruised, there's nothing the hospital can do anyway, even if they are broken, other than give you some pain killers. Go and see your family doctor, he'll sort you out. In the meantime I'll give you a couple of my Ibuprofen 600's that should take the edge off for a while. Take one now and another in the morning but get to see the doctor, soon as.'

'Thanks, I will.'

Harry goes up to his bedroom where he finds his Ibuprofen and goes back to fill a glass of water in the kitchen. Charlie is lying back on the sofa holding his side, looking very sorry for himself. He hands the boy a pill and the glass of water, he grimaces as he sits up again.

'Thanks Harry.' Then swallows the pill and drinks all of the water.

'Would you like a tot of whisky, just to help calm your nerves?'

'Dad wouldn't like it.'

'Dad's not here is he?'

'Okay, that's that would be nice.' Charlie gives him a half smile through his pain. Harry goes to the cupboard in the kitchen where he keeps a bottle of scotch and pours a small tot for Charlie and another for himself. Charlie sips the amber liquid while Harry downs his in one go.

'I needed that, what about you? Go on, bottoms up.'

Charlie swallows the whisky and starts to cough, 'Wow that burns!' Harry laughs.

'That's the idea, medicinal effects.' He continues to laugh, Charlie tries to laugh as well but just ends up coughing some more.

'Yeah, medicine.'

'You say it's just you and your dad,' Harry asks him, 'what happened to your mum, did she die?'

'No, she just took off one day about a year ago, no explanation, no note, only took one suitcase.'

'It must be tough, how did your dad take it?'

'Didn't even cry, reported it to the police but they couldn't find any trace of her either, it's still an open missing person file.'

'I'm really sorry mate, you must really miss her.'

'Yeah, I do, dad thinks she went off with another man.'

'Does he, did he have someone in mind?'

'No, he just said that's what she must have done as she took so little with her.'

'What's her name?'

'Christine, anyway I'd better get off now, thanks for patching me up, I'll go to the doc in the morning, promise.'

'You do that and keep away from Pete and his mates, you're better than they are.'

'I'll try but you should watch your back, he won't like you getting the better of him, he's lost face with the others now.'

'I know, I've known a few like him in my life, I've got the better of most of them and some have got the better of me.' With that he runs his finger along the scar on his face.

'What happened?' Charlie asks

'That's a story for another day, you get off home now and my door is always open to you if you need me.'

'Thanks Harry, be seeing you.' Harry winks and lets him out. After the door shuts Harry goes back to the bottle of scotch and pours another large glass which also goes down in one go. He shakes his head and pours another, smaller one, takes it into the lounge and flops down on the sofa.

'Getting too old for all this Harry my man, far too old.' Suddenly he feels the pain in his tooth return. 'Fuck it, forgot the anti-biotics.'

He goes back to the kitchen draw where he'd put the tablets, takes one out and swallows it dry, then goes back to the sofa.

'Not supposed to drink with these am I?'
He takes another sip of the scotch and closes his eyes.

15.

The next morning the sun is shining, despite being very cold, Harry has the garage door open as he continues to work on his scooter.

'Hello hurray what a nice day for the Eaton Rifles, Eaton Rifles.' Harry sings along to the Jam CD he has playing. 'Hello Hurray I hope rain stops play for the Eaton Rifles, Eaton Rifles.'

He is lost in the music, his thoughts on the job in hand. He doesn't notice someone standing just outside looking in. After a few moments he begins to sense the presence of someone standing watching him. Nonchalantly he reaches over to pick up a large spanner before turning to face the intruder.

'What are you doing?' Charlie asks as Harry is about to take a swing at him with the spanner.

'You shouldn't creep up on people like that, especially after yesterday, you could have found yourself wearing this spanner.'

'Sorry, didn't think, so, what are you doing?'

'Creating a masterpiece sculpture, what does it look like?'

'Yeah, a sculpture.'

'Very funny, come on in.' Harry stands up to pause the CD.

'Don't turn it off, I like The Jam.'

'You know The Jam?'

'Yeah my dad has a greatest hits CD.'

'Sounds like a top man your dad.' Harry turns the CD back on as 'Eaton Rifles' continues to play but turns the volume down a few notches. 'Perhaps I should meet him.' Charlie doesn't respond.

'I've never seen you riding a bike.'

'Bike? Wash your mouth out boy, this is not a bike, they're for Greasers, Rockers. This is a scooter, a Lambretta in fact. This is a GP/DL 200, top of the range for this model and almost fifty years old.'

'A scooter, aren't they a bit, you know…….' Charlie shuffles his feet and looks away from Harry with a half-smile on his face.'

'What?'

'Well, you know, wimpy.'

'WIMPY? Did you say WIMPY?' Harry shakes the spanner at Charlie. 'You can sod off boy.' Charlie laughs.

'Don't get your knickers in a twist, I'm only joking.'

'Wimpy, Jesus wept.' Harry mutters and turns back to the scooter. 'What did your dad say about the bruises?'

'Not much, he doesn't take much notice of what I do.'

'How long has your mum been gone?'

'I told you, about a year now.'

'Right, she's never made any attempts to contact you, birthday card, phone call, Christmas card?'

'Nothing.'

'Have you tried to find her?'

'I wouldn't know where to start.'

'You don't think it's strange, her mother, your grandparents, if they're still alive, don't they know?

'They probably do but I don't know where they live anymore and maybe they don't want my dad to know where she is.'

'Why would that be, did he used to hit her?' Charlie starts to look angry.

'What's it got to do with you anyway?'

'Nothing, mate, nothing, sorry I shouldn't have asked, you're right it's none of my business.'

'No worries, I'll be seeing you around.'

'Wait a minute, how are the ribs?'

'Still a bit sore, you were right, I went to see the doc this morning. The ribs aren't broken just badly bruised, he wanted to know how I did it.'

'And what did you say?' Harry narrowed his eyes questioningly.

'I said I'd fallen down the stairs.'

Harry laughed.

'I'm sure he believed that one.'

'Yeah he didn't look convinced.' Charlie replied, 'anyway, thanks again for last night.'

'No problem, remember, my door is always open to you.' Harry hesitates for a second, 'look after yourself Charlie.'

Charlie nods, waits for a few seconds looking as if he is about to say something else but turns and leaves without saying anything more. Harry sat back on the scooter with a pensive look to watch him walk away.

16

Terry felt like a day off, he'd finished the all the services that were due for collection in the morning so decided he would close up the workshop and take a ride into town. It was a sunny day, cold but sunny, so he took his bike and parked up on the front near the pier. He had no particular plan, maybe a pint somewhere but decided he'd take a walk up the pier, he hadn't done that for a while.

The wind was bracing by the time he arrived at the end by the fun fair. There were a number of anglers hoping for a bite, not something Terry ever fancied doing because he didn't have the patience. After lighting a cigarette he leant on the rails to gaze out to sea, looking for nothing in particular. It wasn't the ideal day for anyone to take a boat out from the Marina, the sea was a bit choppy, but he spotted a small yacht bouncing on the waves heading Christ knows where. He had to laugh at the thought of whoever was on board being struck by sea sickness. Although, if they were seasoned sailors, they were probably managing perfectly well.

Back in the day, when he was a teenager, he'd worked on the fun fair at the end of the pier. The ghost train had been the best ride, the girls would pretend to be scared and he would pretend to calm them down. He'd had quite a few heavy petting moments in the ghost train, happy days.

He finished the cigarette and flicked the butt out to sea but the wind caught it and brought it back past his face. Suddenly Terry felt the cold so turned up the collar on his jacket and made his way back down the pier in search of the pint he had promised himself. Hoping he might bump into a friend who fancied a frame or two of pool, he quickened his step. As he arrived back at the promenade he saw someone that made him stop in his tracks. He hadn't seen that face for some time. Stepping back he partially hid himself beside the candyfloss stand. Watching as the man made his way past the end of the pier towards the town he started to think of the first time he met him.

It was back in the days when he rode with the Rockers, well he was still a Rocker at heart but the days of punch ups on the beach were long gone. Especially after his encounter with this guy, he had just seen, ended with him doing some time in jail. Even if he did deserve it the memory still rankled. If it hadn't been for his father he may well have gone totally off the rails.

That day had been a hot one and the gang had decided to ride into Brighton, maybe have a couple of beers, frighten some tourists and have a paddle. As they rode along Marine Parade Terry, at the front of the gang, spotted a group of scooters parked up there and waved the others to pull up.

'Hey look guys, maybe there's a few Mods in town, what say we go find them and give them the bums rush.'

'They're probably down on the beach or up on the pier, maybe ride along the prom first, we'll be able to see down onto the beach from there.' Terry's friend Jerry suggested.

'Good idea.' Terry agreed. There were eight of them in all and dressed head to toe in leathers. Their machines roared off down towards the promenade in search of the Mods and it wasn't to invite them for a beer.

At the same time Harry and the others are enjoying themselves playing tag around The Lanes. Laughing as they rampage through groups of tourists, pinching girl's arses, and grabbing the occasional one for a kiss. They all stop for a moment being out of breath, laughing and panting at the same time.

'How about we head down to the beach?' Steve suggests, 'Grab some rays.'

'Yeah maybe we can find those girls again.' Frank adds.

'What, and have another ice cream rammed in my face?' They all laugh at the memory. 'No thanks.'

'There'll be plenty more where they came from.' Harry remarks.

'I thought we were going to have a beer.' Says Ed.

'Later Edward dear boy, later.' Steve replies, 'Let's check out the talent first.' Ed doesn't look convinced but follows the others anyway. Steve heads off towards two girls in short skirts who can't see him coming up behind them. He grabs the arse of the one with the long blond hair who lets out a loud yelp and turns to land a heavy slap to his face. Steve reels back from the blow but Harry just managed to catch him as he started to fall.

'You piece of shit!' the girl shouts and moves forward with the intention of planting a fist on his nose. Harry pushes the dazed Steve behind him and holds up a hand towards the blond.

'Hold on, I apologise profusely for my ignorant friend, we don't see such beautiful women where we come from and he was blinded by yours. The blond stops short of thumping Harry, instead she stands back to look him up and down.

'I accept your apology but I want to hear it from him as well, that kind of behaviour may be all right where you come from but it's not acceptable here in Brighton.'

Harry lets Steve go and indicates silently that he should do just that.

'I am so sorry madam,' he sweeps a bow, removing an invisible hat at the same time as he makes his apology.

'I should think so too.'

'Can we buy you a drink?' Harry asks.

'No way!' With that she turned on her heel and stalked off in the opposite direction, her friend shrugged her shoulders and followed without saying a word.'

'Try not to get us arrested for assault.' Frank says sounding pissed off.

'What assault? I was just being friendly.'

'Tell that to the judge. Come on let's have that beer, I'm not sure you'd be safe on the beach.' Ed chipped in. Harry puts his palm on Steve's back with a disapproving look, and pushes him away.

'I think Ed has a point, come on we're here for some fun not to get arrested or piss off the locals.' Steve goes to open his mouth, 'or the tourists. Now move, I saw a pub on the corner.'

With a fast paced stride they rush down the road and around the corner. The boys are laughing until they suddenly see the motorcycle gang are sitting on their machines whilst supping a pint. The boys stop in their tracks, but too late, Terry has seen them.

'Shit!' Bernie exclaims, 'let's back up and go another way.'

'No worries lads, Harry replies, 'they're just having a beer as well. Don't turn around, that would be a mistake, so we'll walk past and find somewhere else to drink.'

'Are you sure about that?' Steve says nervously.

'I am!' Harry replies confidently at which point Terry dismounts and comes over to them to stand in front of Harry

'Looks like you boys have taken a wrong turn.' Terry quips.

'It's a free country.' Steve mutters from behind Harry.'

'Is that so?' Terry laughs as one of the other Rockers comes up to stand beside him.

'You look lost, where did you leave your hairdryers?' the rest of the Rockers start to laugh, 'hope they're safe.' They all laugh again.

'We don't want any trouble.' Frank calls out, 'we're just out for a relaxing day and a couple of pints, like you.'

'But, it could be we want some trouble.'

'Look, we're just going on our way.' Harry says, 'we'll find somewhere else to drink.' Harry starts to move around Terry who forcefully puts his right index finger on Harry's chest.

'Not yet.' Harry looks down at the finger and takes a step back.

17.

Harry continues on his way, unaware of Terry watching him from across the road as he makes his way in the direction of the Royal Pavilion along Old Steine. For a moment he wonders where Harry is going, it had been some time since they saw each other. They'd never been, nor were they ever likely to be, friends. When Terry was sure that Harry had no chance of seeing him he extracted himself from behind the candy floss stand. With one last look in Harry's direction he continued on his mission for a pint and a game of pool.

Harry was on a mission himself, to the police station in John Street where he presented himself to the front desk. The desk sergeant broke into a smile when he saw Harry.

'Harry York, as I live and breathe, long time no see, how are you keeping these days?'

'Getting older and no wiser.'

'How about you Sergeant Miller?'

'Closer to retirement every day.'

'How long have you got to go?'

'Next April, what about you, still on the buses?'

'Sore point, I developed a sleeping problem so I'm not allowed to drive anymore, well, not a bus full of people anyway. I keep looking for another job but at my age the only thing that seems to be on offer is a zero contract with B&Q, not my thing.'

'Sorry to hear that mate, so what can I do for you?'

'Is Inspector Lewis in?'

'You mean Chief Inspector Taylor? Don't let him hear you call him Lewis.'

'Can't help it, he's a Geordie as well, I can only see him as Inspector Lewis now, although I did know him when he was plain PC Lewis'

'On your head be it.' Miller laughs as he picks up the phone and calls through to the CID office, asks for Taylor and puts it back down again. 'He's on his way down, any problems?'

'No, nothing serious, just hoping he can help me with something.'

Harry takes a seat to wait patiently.

Chief Inspector Taylor, a tall thirty something with thinning hair, arrives quickly and ushers Harry into an interview room.

'Good to see you Harry,' Taylor indicates the chair for Harry to sit on. 'I hear you had to leave the buses, hope you're keeping well.'

'I'm fine just can't drive buses anymore.'

'What can I do for you, not in trouble are you?'

'No, not me, there's a young lad living nearby, Charlie Conrad, about fifteen, sixteen, he got into an altercation with a gang of arseholes that I had to extract him from.'

'Did many of them walk away unscathed?' Taylor laughs.

'They all did, what do you take me for?' Harry laughs.

'Well, there was a time.'

'Many moons ago, anyway, he was telling me his mother just upped and disappeared a year or so ago, name of Christine Conrad, do you know anything about it?'

'No mate, we get a lot of missing persons, reports here, especially women. They're usually beaten wives who turn up in a hostel somewhere or have run off with a boyfriend. Sadly not much effort goes into finding them. It's rare for them to vanish without a trace, would you like me to check out the file? If we've got one that is.'

'I'd really appreciate it, the boy is really suffering, and he told me his father reported her missing.'

'No problem, I'll call you, still on the same number?'

'Still on the same number, thanks, Inspector Lewis.'

'I've warned you about that.' Taylor looks stern, shakes his finger under Harry's nose and laughs. 'Only you can get away with it, but not in front of the others, anyway I'm *Chief* Inspector Lewis now.'

'Never dear boy, never.' Harry laughs then gets up to leave.

'Do you need a lift home, I'll see if a patrol car is going you're way?'

'That's all right Ritchie, thanks, I'm going for a coffee with Rita, you should drop in and see her sometime, and she'd be pleased to see you.'

'Yeah, I'll do that Harry, how is she?'

'Actually, she's really good, how about Marianne?'

'Expecting.'

'Really! Wow! Jeez I'm so pleased for you, at last. Give her a hug from me.'

'I will but you should come up to the house sometime, she'd love to see you, bring Rita as well.'

'I'd like that and I'm sure Rita would too. Anyway when is the baby due?'

'Next month.'

'Do you know.....?'

'A girl.'

'Lucky you, would have loved to have a daughter.'

They go quiet for a few seconds.

'Yeah,' Ritchie speaks softly, 'Look sorry mate I have to go, lots on my plate at the moment. I'll be in touch as soon as I can.'

Harry had first met the young, twenty five year old Richie Taylor ten years before when he had first come to Brighton, from Newcastle, as a Detective Constable. Harry had been working a late shift when a youth had attempted to mug him on his way to his car This had been a huge mistake as he didn't know Harry had some training in Ishinryru karate, not a lot but enough. In no time he'd disarmed the boy and called the police.

It was Ritchie Taylor who arrived on the scene and they struck up a friendship. They would often have drinks together, not so much recently, since Ritchie had married Marianne; he had attended the wedding and they had kept in touch. He was a good copper and had risen through the ranks to become a Chief Inspector only last year. Harry was as proud of him as he would be if he was his son.

Harry waved him goodbye as he left the station to make his way back to Rita's café which he managed in fifteen minutes. As soon as he came through the door Sara started to make his coffee, it was quite busy in there.

'Rita's out back, up to her elbows in onions, want to go through? I'll bring you the coffee when it's ready.' Sara said.

'Yeah, thanks Sara.'

True enough Rita was busily chopping onions, with a bowl of tomatoes waiting for her to get to as well. She smiled as Harry came through the bamboo curtains.

'How did you get on, did you see Ritchie?'

'Yeah, he didn't know anything about it, didn't think he would really but he said he would dig out the file, if there is one.'

'This lad has really got to you hasn't he?'

'He has, first of all I don't like bullies and second.......' Harry pauses, 'and second he misses his mum and I'm not convinced his dad is such a good guy, just a vibe I'm getting.' Sara pops her head in the kitchen and hands him the coffee.

'Thanks darling,'

'Do you want a BLT to go with that?' Rita asks.

'No thanks, I'll finish the coffee then I need to get back home.'

'What have you got on?'

'I uncovered the Lambretta and I've been working on it.'

'Really?' Rita's eyes widened. 'How long has it been since it last saw the light of day?'

'Too long.'

'What prompted this move?' Rita asked looking sideways at Harry, who didn't respond. 'Oh I know. It's this lad you rescued, he really has got under your skin hasn't he?' She wipes her eye with the back of her hand and instantly regrets it as the essence of onion seeps in. 'Oh, ouch, that was a mistake.'

As tears start to well up in her eye Harry takes out a tissue and wipes them away.

'Is that the onions or....?'

'Just the onions you old fool! The scooter eh, you going to put it back on the road?'

'That's the idea, maybe I'll give you a ride, what do you say?'

'I'm not a young girl anymore Harry.'

'I'm no spring chicken either darling, so, what do you say?' She leans back against the chopping block.

'Seriously?'

'Seriously, well, if you can lend me the money to tax and insure it.'

Rita laughs and throws the onion at him that was in her hand, narrowly missing his head as he ducks to avoid it.

'You, what am I going to do with you?'

18

Harry enjoyed his walk home, it wasn't a short distance but he liked to keep himself as fit as possible at his age. About half way the clouds began to roll over and get darker and darker. Hoping he could get back before the heavens opened Harry quickened his pace. Unfortunately with just five minutes to go before reaching the safety of his house the heavens opened and the rain fell from the skies.

'Bugger!' Exclaimed Harry as be broke into a trot, 'couldn't you have waited a few more minutes?' He shouts to no one in particular.

Once back in the house he towel dries his hair and proceeds to make himself a cup of tea. Just as he is dipping a digestive biscuit into it Harry notices the light flashing on his answer machine. Curiously he hits the play button to hear the voice of Ritchie Taylor.

'Hi Harry, I guess you're still on your way home as I tried you at Rita's. Give me a bell when you have a chance I managed to find some information on the elusive Christine Conrad.'

'So soon,' Harry mutters to himself as he warms his hands on the cup of tea then picks up the phone to return Taylor's call. Unfortunately, when he got through to the CID office he's too late, as Ritchie had left the building and wasn't expected back for some time. He decided to wait until later rather than call his mobile, in case it was an inconvenient moment.

Instead he decided to go back to work on the scooter. Although it was still raining cats and dogs Harry opened the garage door for ventilation as he hoped to get the engine running soon, so put his coat back on. With just a few parts to put back he then re-attached the panels. While standing back to admire the beauty of the Lambretta, a smile of remembrance came over his face. There had been a lot of happy memories associated with this machine, and a few bad ones, he remembers as he once again absentmindedly ran his finger over his scar.

'Maybe a small glass of whisky to celebrate.' With that he goes back into the house to pour one. When he returns to the garage he finds Charlie standing over the scooter.

'It's looking good Harry, when are you going to ride it?'

'Have to get it taxed and insured first, so how are you today?'

'My ribs are hurting quite a bit even though I managed to get some strong pain killers from the doctor.'

'It'll be quite a while before they heal, I know from bitter experience.'

'Did you get a kicking as well then?'

'Not exactly, I came off the scooter once and slammed into a lamppost, it wasn't funny, although I have had more than my fair share of fights.'

'Is that where you got the scar? From a fight I mean not the lamp post.'

'Yeeeeah.'

'Really? Wow, tell me about it.'

'Some other time, it's not something I like to think about.'

'But.....'

'Some other time I said.' Charlie shrugs his shoulders and says no more about it. 'I've actually been waiting for you.'

'Me?'

'Yeah.'

'Look, you're an old man and I'm a teenager, is this some sort of come on? I mean I'm...'

'I'll pretend I didn't hear that.' Harry turns away and goes back to the scooter. Charlie's face reddens in embarrassment when he realises he has offended Harry.

'Look Harry, I'm sorry, I mean I don't really know you and you hear about this sort of, I mean, oh shit you know what I mean.'

Harry grunts but keeps his back to him.

'You got homework to do?'

'No it's done.' Harry turns back to face him.

'Why did you come here?'

'I was on my way to meet someone when I saw your garage door open. You weren't there, I thought someone might take something from here.'

'That was thoughtful of you, who were you going to meet?'

'Pete.' Harry stands up and narrows his eyes as he looks at Charlie.

'You can't be serious, that twat from the other day, the one you're still carrying the bruises for?' Charlie chuckles.

'Yeah, the twat from the other day.'

'Why on earth do you want to go and meet him?'

'Well, he's sort of a friend.'

'A friend? With friends like that you don't need enemies.'

'I don't find it so easy to make friends.'

'I'm not surprised if you hang around with him, decent people wouldn't want to be involved with that sort of twat and if you are, they will give you a wide berth.'

Charlie looks embarrassed and turns away.

'I guess you're right, it's just, since mum left I don't seem to be to...... oh I don't know.'

'Don't you have friends at school?'

'Yeah but most of them live the other side of town.'

'Not easy is it?'

Harry's question hangs in the air.

'So, are you going to start her up?' Charlie says, changing the subject.

'That's the idea.'

Harry looks uncertain but turns back to straddle the machine, takes a deep breath and kicks down the starter. Nothing happens, 'Try it again.' Charlie encourages him, Harry looks up with a grimace then tries once more. This time the engine tries to start, so, encouraged Harry tries again, but this time it makes a screeching sound so Harry stops it.

'Have you cleaned the spark plug and checked the gap?'

'Do you know about scooters?' Harry asks.

'No but I know a bit about engines, so have you?'

'Yes I have.'

'What about the points, clean them as well?'

'Ahh, maybe not.'

'Get off, let me have a look.' Harry moves away from the machine whilst Charlie removes his coat, rolls up his sleeves then proceeds to remove the side panel to get at the distributor. After removing the cap he turns back to Harry, 'do you have any sandpaper?'

'Somewhere,' Harry starts to search through the drawers in the bench at the back of the garage. 'Voila!' He pulls out a small, used piece of sandpaper and hands it to Charlie who uses it carefully on the points. When he is satisfied Charlie replaces the distributor cap and stands up.

'OK try it again.' Charlie wipes his hands as he steps away from the scooter then waves his left arm majestically towards it for Harry.

'Thank you dear boy.'

Harry straddles the machine once more and kicks down the starter once more. Again it makes a brave attempt to start but it soon becomes quite obvious there is something seriously wrong with it.

'I think it's a bit more serious than the points.' Charlie observes, 'in fact I have a suspicion that the engine may have seized, has it been standing here for long?'

'Hmmm yes,' Harry chuckles, 'a year or ten,'

'Same petrol in the tank?'

'For sure.'

'Petrol is useless after about seven years so that won't help, but I still think the engine might be seized.

'So it's fucked then?

'Is that a technical term?' They both laugh.

'You could say that.' Harry replied.

'You need a whole new engine.'

'Yeah I thought that might be the case.'

'Where do you find one for a dinosaur like this?'

'Careful, there are quite a few Lambretta specialists on line but a new engine is an arm and a leg more than I have.' A thought suddenly comes into Harry's head causing a wry smile to spread over his face. 'However, I might just have the chance to get one.'

'Really, Where?'

'Don't you worry, leave it to me.'

'What about the rest of it?'

'What do you mean?'

'It looks like it could do with a clean-up.'

'What! I spent ages on it the other day.'

'Maybe but do you want it to be clean or do you want it to really sparkle?'

Harry sits back on the scooter, puts his head on one side but doesn't speak for a few moments while Charlie shuffles his feet.

'Well?'

'You're right, it could look amazing, fancy helping?'

'What do you mean?'

'What I said, do you fancy helping me get it back to what it should be?'

'Why would you want me to help?'

'Well, other than you seem to know your way around an engine and my hands and eyes are not what they were. Plus, I hate to see a good kid waste his time hanging around with the likes of Pete.'

'He's…. 'Charlie goes to say something.

'Don't!' Harry holds up a hand, 'Don't try and tell me he's not that bad really, how are your ribs?' Charlie rubs his side subconsciously at the thought. 'And maybe it would be good if you apply yourself to something you might be interested in.'

Charlie looks away pensively, his eyes settle on a photograph pinned to the wall and walks over for a closer look. It's Harry sitting on the scooter, wearing a Zoot suit and looking a lot younger than he does now.

'Is that you?'

'Yeah, back in the day.'

'You're looking pretty cool.'

'Well, thank you.'

'Stylish……………almost.'

'Cheek,' Harry pretends to swipe his hand across Charlie's face. 'So, yes or no? Unless you want to get another kicking from the genial Pete.'

'I can't today but if you want I'll pop by after school tomorrow.'

'That would be fab, I'll have the kettle on.'

Charlie smiles, as does Harry, then starts to walk away but stops in his tracks and turns back.

'On one condition.' Says Charlie.

'What's that?'

'I get to have a ride when it's finished.'

'Deal!' Harry strides over to Charlie and shakes his hand.

'Deal.' Charlie smiles and makes his way home, Harry watches as he walks away down the street then suddenly he remembers something.

'Bugger, Ritchie.' He quickly closes the garage door and makes his way back into the house where he picks up the phone and dials the number of the police station. 'Hello, Harry York here, can I speak to Chief Inspector Taylor please?'

After a few seconds he came on the line.

'Harry, I tried calling yesterday, there was a file on Christine Conrad and it would appear we did manage to track her down.'

'Really, what happened to her?'

'It would seem after a lot of physical abuse she went to a women's shelter in Shoreham, the husband traced her there and tried to remove her. This was unsuccessful and she managed to find a new life in Eastbourne.'

'Didn't she try and take her son with her?'

'I don't know about that, all I know is she asked that we didn't give her husband any information as to her whereabouts.'

'What about her son, did she say not to give him any information?'

'Nothing in the file about that.'

'Can you give me an address?'

'I don't know Harry, I don't think I can, not without getting her permission at least.'

'Do you think you could speak to her for me? I mean Charlie thinks she ran off with another man, doesn't she think he deserves to know the truth? Tell her I'll come and speak to her before I say anything to her son.'

'For you Harry, I'll make contact, have you spoken to the father?'

'I've not met him, yet, but I fully intend to, in the not too distant future, I'll let you know what I think of him. Did you have any dealings with him?'

'No, like I said, it wasn't my case.'

'Thanks for your help Ritchie and let me know what she says.'

'I will.' With that Harry hangs up and sits back thoughtfully.

19.

True to his word, after school Charlie comes by to help Harry strip the engine down once again. He really seemed to know what he was doing, so much so they could see their faces in many of the parts as if they were mirrors.

'Not looking bad, you have a talent there.'

'I used to polish my great grandad's medals, kind of reminded me of it.'

'Is he still with us?' Harry enquired.

'No, he died when I was very young, dad just wanted me to clean them so he could put them up for sale.'

'Which one of the forces was he in, Army, Navy, Air Force?'

'Army.'

'You must be proud of him.'

'Yeah, sort of.'

'What do you mean?'

'Nothing.' Charlie looked back to the scooter and fiddled with nothing in particular, Harry didn't push him.

'My grandfather was in the army during the first war while my dad was in the navy the second time around, they're both long gone too.'

'I have to say this finish is looking pretty good.' Charlie says changing the subject.'

'Yeah the kids' are all right.' Harry starts to sing.

'What?' Charlie says looking puzzled.

'The Kids are All Right, by The Who.'

'The what?'

'The Who!'

'Who what?' Harry laughs.

'Don't tell me you've never heard of The Who!'

'Is it a band?'

'It's THE band, come over here.' Harry takes him to the shelf full of vinyl albums where he pulls out Quadrophenia, Tommy and Who's Next. 'There's power in these records, a kind of alchemy like the Holy Grail for generations of Mods.'

'Mods? I've heard my granddad talk about Mods, didn't they smash up the beach years ago?'

'Yeah, but not just them.' Harry replies, 'they had a bit of help from the Rockers.' Harry laughs.

Charlie looks along the spines of Harry's album collection.

'I've never heard of any of these, except maybe The Beatles, oh and The Rolling Stones.'

'Then I'm about to open your ears to a brave new world.' With that he pulls out the CD of Tommy, puts it in the machine and hits the play button. 'I'll tell you what, there's a Who covers band playing the Concord club at the weekend, do you fancy coming with me?'

'Er yeah maybe.'

'Run it past your dad, check he's OK with it.'

'He won't care.'

'Well, run it past him anyway.'

'Run what past him?' a voice comes from behind them at the garage door. 'I've been looking for you boy, your tea's ready.' Standing in the doorway is a man, maybe in his late thirties, with close cropped hair and a five o'clock shadow. Harry moves forward, holding his hand out in greeting.

'Hi, you must be Charlie's dad, pleased to meet you. I'm Harry.' Charlie's father hesitates then takes his hand, Harry thought there was something familiar about him but couldn't quite think what it might be.

'Brian. So what are you running past me?'

'Well Charlie has been helping me with my scooter - I'm trying to get it going again.'

'Has he?'

'Yes, he saw me working on it and we got chatting.' Harry guessed that the boy hadn't told his father anything about being beaten by Pete and co. Charlie shot him a thank you look. 'I've been playing him some of my old Who albums, he seems to like them so as a thank you for his help I thought it might be nice to take him to see Who's Who at the Concord on Saturday. Of course, if that's all right with you.' Brian looks back and forth from Harry to Charlie.

'Fine by me, if that's what he wants to do.' He looks pointedly towards Charlie, who shuffles his feet with making any comment.

'Yeah it sounds great.'

'So that's fixed then.' Harry smiles, 'better get off for your tea then Charlie, I'll see you before the weekend?'

'Sure thing Harry.' Charlie picks up his coat and starts to walk away, Brian doesn't move but looks sideways at Harry.

'Thanks for looking out for him, I hope he hasn't been a nuisance.'

'Far from it, he's been a great help.' Brian glances over the scooter parts and the records in Harry's hands, looking a little uncertain.

'Well you take care, and have a nice evening.'

'Thanks, I will, after I've cleaned up here, and you have one yourself.'

Brian nods and turns away to leave, Charlie is waiting for him a bit further along the road. Harry watches the two of them as they walk down the road. He notices the way Brian grips Charlie's neck with his hand until they turn the corner out of sight. Harry narrows his eyes thinking it was strange Brian hadn't mentioned seeing any bruises on his son. Charlie obviously hadn't told him about the beating he'd received from Pete and his cronies. Perhaps the father hadn't noticed them among the others he had given him. If he'd been beating Charlie's mother and she had gone, maybe he'd diverted his anger towards his son.

'I'll have to keep an eye on you sunshine.' Harry mutters to himself, then closes the garage doors to turn back to the scooter. 'Ah I can't be bothered.' Instead of clearing up he turns up the volume on the Tommy CD and skips to 'Pinball Wizard' where he proceeds to play air guitar.

A man alone, a man out of time.

'A man in need of a drink.' Harry laughs and makes his way back into house to find the bottle of whisky. He picks it up and turns it around in his hand thoughtfully. 'Maybe not today Harry, a cup of tea instead.'

He puts the bottle back and goes into the kitchen where he switches the kettle on to make himself tea, then picks up the phone to dial a number. After it rings three times Rita's voice answers.

'What are you doing Saturday evening?'

21.

It's the open road and Harry can feel the wind blowing through his hair as he speeds along the country lane on his scooter. With no cloud in the sky the sun is beating down on his face whilst being cooled by the wind. There's no other car, bike or even a pedestrian to be seen, so he opens up the throttle taking the dial of the speedo round as far as it will go. Fields and trees flash by in a blur as Harry sings at the top of his voice.

'Born to be wi-i-i-i-ild!' He rounds a bend, far too fast, loses control and comes off the road into a tree with a sickening crunch as his skull makes contact with the aforementioned tree trunk.

The world is spinning, round and round, getting faster. The heat from the sun is getting more intense, he can't move as his legs are pinned down by the scooter. The heat from the engine is burning through his jeans to flay the skin from his bones, then…….

A bell rings in his head, it's getting louder and louder. Harry opens his eyes to look around his bedroom then to the clock that reads eight thirty.

'A bloody dream,' someone is swinging on the doorbell so he sits up to put his legs out of the bed, stand and make his way over to the window. 'All right, all right give it a rest.' Harry opens the window to look down where he sees Charlie looking back up to him.

'Don't you have school to go to?' Harry enquires.

'Half term.' Charlie replies.

'I thought that started on Monday.'

'Yeah, it does.' Harry smiles.

'Does your dad know you're not at school?'

'Yeah.'

'Of course he does, wait there I'll be down in a minute.' With that Harry closes the window and reaches for his dressing gown. After a quick visit to the bathroom he makes his way downstairs to open the door. Charlie steps inside and waits in the hall to be invited into the lounge. 'Go on in and take a pew, if you can find one that is, I haven't tidied up for a few days, to be honest I live like a pig, single man and all that.'

'No worries, my dad's not much better and my room's a bit of a mess too.'

Charlie rubs his neck absent mindedly, Harry notices an angry looking bruise there. Charlie becomes aware of what he's doing and that Harry is noticing it so he pulls the collar of his coat up in an attempt to cover it. Harry makes no comment.

'What's on the agenda for today?' Harry doesn't respond immediately, 'Harry?'

'Well, before I can think about that I need a cup of tea so I'm going to put the kettle on, you want one?'

'Yes please, two sugars.'

'Sugar's bad for you, should try tea without it and it tastes a whole lot better.'

'Nah, I've tried it and didn't like it.'

'Might have a problem there, I'm out of sugar.'

'Never mind I'll leave it then.'

'I've got some juice if you like.'

'Yes please, that would be great.' Harry puts the kettle on for his tea and gives Charlie a glass of orange juice. When the tea is made Harry turns on the TV and looks at Charlie's bruise again but still says nothing about it.

'I'm just going for a shower, then later I have to go somewhere, do you fancy a trip?'

'You mean like a road trip?'

'Yeah but don't get too excited, it's not that far.'

'You haven't got a car, have you?'

'No, but I know someone who does.' Harry smiles, picks up his tea and makes his way to the stairs. 'Watch a bit of TV, I'll be back soon, help yourself to more juice and make some toast if you want.'

'I'm fine thanks.' Charlie replies.

Harry nods and makes his way upstairs while Charlie flips around the channels, Harry only has a Freeview box so there isn't much on other than news and breakfast TV. When he can't find anything he wants to watch Charlie starts to look around at all the photographs on the wall. Many of them are of a young Harry with his scooter or a guitar.

Eventually he sees a frame with four small pictures of a boy of about six or seven years old. They are obviously taken at different times, one has him standing by a Christmas tree with a teddy bear in his hands. Charlie removes it from the wall for a closer look and turns it over to see 'Sammy 1989'. Making a mental to ask Harry about it later Charlie replaces it on the wall and goes back to watching the TV. As there is still nothing much to see he takes out his phone, plugs some earplugs in and searches for some music to listen to. Turning the music up loud he isn't aware of Harry returning, all washed and scrubbed up.

'What are you listening too?' Harry asks but Charlie clearly doesn't hear him so Harry shouts out. 'I said, what are you listening too?' This time it makes Charlie jump and then he removes the speakers from his ears.

'Sorry I didn't hear you come in, er it's Tinie Tempah.'

'Oh yeah, surprisingly I have heard of him, not my sort of thing but whatever floats your boat. Hopefully I can get you into The Who and other similar bands.'

'Well I am giving Who's Who a go tomorrow aren't I?'

'That you are young man, that you are.'

'You're looking smart today, where are we going.'

'Not far, to the daughter of a friend of mine.'

'What for?'

'You'll see, something that could be beneficial to us both.'

Just as he makes his way over to sit on the sofa the doorbell rings, Charlie looks nervous.

'Who's that?'

'Don't worry, I'm pretty sure it's our ride.' Charlie looks puzzled as Harry goes to answer it. Rita is standing on the doorstep to be ushered into the lounge by Harry. She gives him a peck on the cheek as she squeezes past him into the room.

'Hello,' Rita says with surprise as she sees Charlie sitting on the sofa.

'Hello.' Charlie replies whilst standing up.

'Who's your sidekick Harry?' Rita asks.

'My name's Charlie.' He tells her with a note of indignation in his voice.

'Sorry love, I didn't mean to offend you.'

'It's OK.' Charlie looks embarrassed. Harry shoots her a look and she realises he's the boy Harry has told her about.

'So how do you know Harry?'

'He lives up the road,' Harry interjects before Charlie can say anything, 'and saw me working on the scooter he's interested in helping. He seems to know quite a bit about engines.'

'Really? Well that sounds, er good. You like tinkering with engines then?'

'Yeah I do.'

'And there's me thinking all teenage boys liked doing was playing computer games and chasing girls.'

'I'm not into computer games.'

'What about girls?' Charlie gives a half smile and a chuckle.

'Don't have a lot of luck there.'

'Awe you will, good looking boy like you, if I were, oh let's say forty years younger………………' Rita puts her arm around his shoulder and they all laugh.

'Forty years?' Harry asks.

'Cheek.' Rita responds and they all laugh again. 'I can see you and I are going to get along Charlie, you coming with us?' Charlie nods, 'Harry?'

'Yeah ready.'

'Come on then, but I need to get some petrol.'

22.

Rita pulls into a petrol station to fill up, Harry and Charlie stay in the car while she does it. When she finishes Rita puts her head into the car.

'Can I get anybody anything from the shop?' She asks.

'Not for me.' Harry answers.

'Wouldn't mind a Coke, please.' Charlie adds.

'A Coke it is.' Rita closes the door, Charlie watches as Rita makes her way over to the kiosk to pay.

'Your friend seems like a nice lady.' Charlie says to Harry without taking his eyes off her.

'That's because she is a nice lady.' Says Harry as he turns to face Charlie who smiles. 'What?' Harry asks.

'Nothing.' Charlie broadens his smile.

'Come on, what's going on in that pea brain of yours?'

'Ho, ho, ho have I hit a nerve?'

'No, I just want to know what you're smiling for.'

'It's nothing,' Charlie continues to smile as he looks back to where Rita is still queuing to pay.

'It's not nothing otherwise you wouldn't have that stupid grin plastered all over your daft face.' Charlie shuffles in his seat and looks back to Harry.

'It's just…….. Well I thought I was crap with girls, but you, you don't seem to have a clue.'

'What do you…..?'

'For an old man.' Charlie interjects before Harry can finish his sentence.

'A clue? Old man?' Harry shakes his head.

'Well, older man, I didn't mean to offend you.'

'That's good, I'll try not to be offended and I hope you won't be offended when I give you a slap.'

'It's just, well the way you look at her.'

'And what way is that?'

'Like the way my mum used to look at my dad before………..' Charlie broke off and looked away.

'Before what Charlie?'

'Never mind.'

'Did your dad beat on your mum?'

'Don't miss out with her.' Charlie ignores Harry's question as he nods towards Rita who is returning to the car.

'It's complicated.'

'Seems pretty simple to me.'

'You boys okay?' Rita gets back in the car and hands the can of Coke to Charlie. 'Off we go then!' She starts the engine and pulls out of the garage.

As they drive Harry and Charlie don't speak leaving an awkward silence in the car.

'You two all right? You're very quiet.'

'Just enjoying the ride.' Charlie replies, Harry looks round at him.

'Yeah, just enjoying the ride.' Harry echoes, Rita shoots him a look but he just raises his eyebrows and goes back to looking out the window. The journey continues in silence until Rita switches on the radio. After a short while she pulls over to consult a map.

'We're getting close, perhaps you can direct me from here.' She hands the map over to Harry. 'This is where we are.' She says stabbing her finger on the map, 'and this is where we need to be.'

'Right,' Harry studies it for a few moments, 'up here and take the third right.' Rita pulls away to take the turning. After a few minutes and directions from Harry, Rita pulls up outside a house.

'Number eleven you said, is that right?'

'That's right, you two stay here I'll check.' Harry gets out of the car and goes up the garden path to the front door. He hesitates for a few minutes, runs his hand over his hair then rings the bell. In a few short moments a young woman of maybe thirty years old holding a baby answers the door.

'Hello, Denise is it?' She smiles.

'Hi, yes, you must be Harry.'

'Hmm yes, that's me.'

'Come in, come in, I kind of remember you from when I was a kid.'

'Yeah but I got old, can I bring my friends with me? Wouldn't have got here without Rita.' Harry nods his head in the direction of the car.

'Sure, the more the merrier.' He waves his hand at Rita and Charlie to indicate they should join him and waits on the doorstep for them.

'This is Rita.'

'Yes I think my dad has mentioned you, you've got a café near the prom in Brighton.'

'That's right, I've known your dad from years back.'

'And who's this, your son?'

'No this is Charlie, Harry seems to have taken him under his wing.'

'Well come on in all of you.'

'I'm helping Harry fix his scooter.' pipes up Charlie. 'I live around the corner', he adds as Denise shows them into the lounge.

'Do you know about scooters then?' she asks him.

'No but I do know a fair bit about engines and he needs a new one.'

'Really.' Denise says whilst looking in Harry's direction.

Charlie is looking around the room noting the vast difference between it and Harry's tip. Other than the baby stuff in the corner it's all neat and tidy with baby pictures on the wall instead of scooters.

'Take a seat, can I make you some tea or coffee?'

'No thanks, we need, well I need to get back to the café I've left my young assistant in charge Not that she can't cope, especially at this time of the year, she can, I just don't like to leave her alone for too long.'

'You saw dad the other day, he told me.'

'Yes I went with the rest of the gang, it was a bit of a shock to see him like that. It's been a while so I couldn't believe how he was looking. Are you going soon?'

'I go every day when my husband gets home from work so he can look after the baby.'

'How old is he, or is it she?' Rita asks.

'He, Simon, four months, I'm glad dad managed to see his grandchild before..............' Denise trails off with tears welling up in her eyes. Rita stands up to comfort her.

'Here let me take him while you find a tissue.' Denise hands the baby to Rita and searches for the tissue in her sleeve. 'Harry and I know how you feel we both lost a parent to cancer, not the same one but it's all much the same pain, with the same result.'

'I hope you don't think we're intruding.' Harry says quietly.

'No, no of course not, you're one of dad's oldest friends, I've heard so many stories about when you were all young, free and single.'

'Ha, I hope not all of them.' Harry laughs

'No really, he insisted I should see you before, well while he's still with us, to make sure I give you want he wants you to have, he said you've got the list.'

'That's right, here.' Harry removes a piece of paper and hands it to Denise who looks it over and smiles.

'Okay, I've got no idea what any of these things are but Dad was always meticulous when it came to labelling all his stuff so it should be pretty easy to find everything. 'Rita do you think you can keep hold of Simon while we go into the garage to find all this stuff?'

'Try and stop me,' she nuzzles her face into the baby's neck, 'he's a beautiful boy, aren't you Simon?' She looks longingly at the baby and suddenly comes overwhelmed with emotion and tears start to well up in her eyes. Harry is looking the other way but Charlie notices.

'Rita, are you all right?' he asks her as she wipes away the tears. Harry reaches out to touch her arm but she pulls away.

'Reet?'

'Yes, I'm fine, don't worry about me, just being a silly old woman.' Harry reaches out again but this time she lets him touch her whilst giving him a half smile and mouths 'I'm okay' silently.

'Do you have any of your own, grand kids?'

Rita doesn't respond for a moment and looks towards Harry again. 'No,' for a second Rita still looks sad then smiles at Denise. 'No I don't.' Denise, looks at Harry who turns away, doesn't pursue it any further.

'Are you all right to come and give me a hand Harry?' He doesn't respond whilst looking a bit dazed, 'Harry?'

'Sure, yes sorry.' Harry snaps out of his reverie,' Show me the way.' He starts to follow her out of the living room but turns back and calls to Charlie. 'Come on we may need another pair of hands.'

Harry gives Rita one more look then follows Denise and Charlie out to the garage.

'Did I touch a nerve there Harry?' Denise asks.

'Yeah, she always wanted to have a child but, well, things don't always work out the way you want them to, do they?'

'Is she married?'

'No, not anymore.'

'I'm sorry I don't mean to be nosey, she just seemed so upset.'

'No worries, she'll be all right.' Denise gives him a half smile.

'You sure about that?' Charlie asks.

'Yes!' Harry snaps back at him and turns back to Denise with a smile. 'Are you all right with me taking all this stuff?'

'Of course, they are my dad's last wishes, anyhow what am I going to do with all these bit of scooters?'

'Well you might want to have one of your own one day.' Harry quips, Denise laughs at the thought.

'Can you imagine me and little Simon on a scooter? No it's what dad wanted. His wish is my command, as they say.'

Harry looks around at the very tidy garage, thinking how much tidier it is than his own, with boxes clearly marked and stacked neatly. He starts to look in them and gets excited at what they contain.

'This is wonderful stuff…..' Harry starts to choke back tears, 'it's almost as if he knew…..'

'Yes it is, but he was only diagnosed a short time ago and he did all this long before then.' She puts her hand on Harry's shoulder in comfort. 'He told me you were great friends.'

'Yeah we were, well, are really. Back in the day we were inseparable. We'd go for rides out to Brighton, as you know we used to live in South London, Lewisham in fact, not the centre of the cosmos. So trips to the coast were great, well most of the time.' He touches his scar remembering something from the past.

'You always remember the good times don't you? I know I do, we also went to see bands play, and being mods we liked all that kind of music, especially The Jam and The Who.'

'Yes I know, one of the items on the list is a box of records, they're over there.' Harry gets up to have a look.

'Wow, The Chords, The Lambrettas, oh and the Merton Parkas, I lost my copies of these years ago.' He pulls out a copy of Secret Affair. 'Bloody hell, this is mine!' He laughs, 'look here my name is on the back, crafty bugger he must have lifted it when I wasn't looking.'

'You must have had quite a life.' Charlie chips in.

'Yes we did, we were the gang of five but like most people we gradually drifted apart, jobs, marriage. You know how it is. It was only Ed and myself who ended up down this neck of the woods. The other three stayed in Lewisham. We used to get together a lot at first but families started to get in the way and we saw less and less of each other. In the last few years it's been an annual event. However, we did all get to visit him in the hospice the other day.'

'Yes, he said you were there, even Steve.' Denise says, which makes Harry laugh. 'I know all about Steve, and mum.'

Harry doesn't make comment.

'Yeah even Steve, there's always been a bit of a love hate relationship with those two. I think that's more love than hate, Steve liked to wind him up and Ed would always rise to the bait not taking it very well. The more he got wound up the more Steve would do it, and I got stuck in the middle. Surprisingly though it never came to blows.' Charlie and Denise laugh.

'He told me he always knew Steve would have his back.'

'Really?' Harry says, somewhat surprised. 'I'm going to miss him you know.'

'Yes I know, I'm going to miss him too.'

'Of course you are darling.' Harry takes a deep breath and stands up. 'Right Charlie old son let's get this stuff into the car.'

'I'll help.' Denise offers.

'Don't be silly, we can manage but perhaps you can go and get the car keys from Rita, if she can bear to tear herself away from your son for a second.'

'Of course I will, you make a start and I'll meet you back outside.' Denise goes back inside the house leaving Harry and Charlie to start getting the boxes out to the car.

'Is Rita really all right Harry, she looked pretty upset?'

'I'm sorry I snapped at you earlier Charlie, it's a long story for another day.'

'Okay, no worries.' Charlie nods and picks up the first box. When they had finished packing Harry and Charlie went back into the house where Rita is still enjoying her time with young Simon.

'Can I get you anything before you leave?' Denise asks.

'No we're find thanks.' Harry replies.

'Maybe I can take this one with me.' Rita quips, Denise laughs while Harry just smiles.

'Don't be strangers, I mean you are always welcome to come and visit, even after…. Well you know what I mean. I'd love to see you all again, and when, I mean after, I mean….' Denise start to cry.

'It's okay sweetheart, we know what you mean.' Harry speaks softly as he puts a comforting arm around her shoulders. 'Of course we'll keep in touch, I've known you since you were knee high to a grasshopper, not going to stop now.'

Denise smiles and pecks Harry on the cheek.

'If you ever need a babysitter.' Rita says as she hands the baby Simon back to his mother, 'I come free, just give me a call, here, let me give you my mobile number.'

'Really? We always have trouble finding someone, not so much trustworthy but who can handle a baby, plenty of young girls want the money but I'm on edge the entire evening so tend not to go out, ever.'

'Well, don't you worry pet, I know how to look after babes.'

Denise shows them to the door where they all hug each other, as Denise hugs Charlie, who seems to enjoy it, she whispers in his ear.

'Look after him for me.'

'I will, he's been very good to me.'

'He's a good man.'

'Yeah, I know.'

Denise waves' goodbye as the car pulls away and wipes away her tears which come on harder and faster. Her body starts to shake while she cries even more. While trying to stifle her crying by burying her face into the baby's neck, she closes her door as the car, with Harry and co, disappears out of sight.

23.

Live music had always been something Harry lived for, ever since he could remember. The first band he ever saw live was, of course, The Jam. He already loved their records and when Steve arrived buzzing with excitement on his doorstep with a bundle of tickets to see them, he buzzed as well. So the gang of five went to see the show at Lewisham Odeon, they were talking about it for weeks afterwards. The night had stayed with him ever since. They all went to see a countless number of gigs featuring an array of bands from the famous down to many whose names had long been consigned to the bin labelled 'can't remember their names.' Most of the time he either went with the gang of five or some of them. Later this might just be a girlfriend but he'd hardly been to see anyone, at least in the last ten years.

The most magical night was the one where he managed to get the Jam to sign his poster.

This night was the first time, in he didn't know how long, and he was looking forward to it. Not just to hear the music, Who's Who were a really good Who tribute act he'd seen once many years before, but he really wanted to turn Charlie on to the music he loved so much. Not to mention Rita would be there too.

The Concorde 2 is one of the leading live venues on the UK club circuit with many bands returning time and time again. It's

84

situated on Madeira Drive which is right on the Brighton sea front. Originally built as tea rooms in the Victorian era it became a bikers café in the 1960's then in the 70's an amusement arcade. It was eventually transformed in 2000 into the fine live venue it is today and has been described as the perfect venue by The Foo Fighters Dave Grohl who played there in 2008.

The weather was still very typical late January, always blowing a gale on the front as Harry, Rita and Charlie queued to get in. They were quite near the front. There was quite a crowd waiting with turned up collars in an attempt to keep the rain out. On the dot of seven the doors opened and in no time the trio found themselves inside jostling at the bar where Harry was attempting to buy a round of drinks, he soon got the attention of the girl behind the bar.

'Hey I know you,' she shouts over the loud music from the DJ. 'You used to drive my bus to school.'

'Those were the days.' Harry replies.

'You threw my mate off for smoking.'

'Did I? Sorry about that.' She laughs.

'No worries, I said it was bad for her.' She laughs again, 'what can I get you?'

'Guinness for me, vodka and orange for the lady and er, what about you Charlie?'

'Pint of lager please.'

'Pint of Coke for my young friend.'

'Coming up.' The girl says and goes off to pull the pint of Guinness.'

'Harry, can't I have a pint?'

'You're fifteen mate, if the old bill came in and saw you the club may well lose its license, and the girl behind the bar could lose her job for selling alcohol to someone underage, is that what you want?'

'Er, well if you put it like that.' Charlie looks sheepish.

'And I do,'

'Then I'm happy with a Coke.'

'Good boy.' Rita adds whilst ruffling his hair. 'You can have a beer back at Harry's after the show, can't he Harry?'

'Of course he can, I've got a few cans in the fridge.'

'Do you have anything for me?'

'Sure, I always keep some wine and a bottle of vodka in case you drop by.'

'Are you being………'

'No, it's true.'

'That'll be eighteen pound please mister bus driver.' The girl behind the bar puts down the drinks and smiles at Harry.

'Harry, my name's Harry.'

'Okay Harry, I hope you're not driving the bus tonight.' She adds as he hands her the money.

'Not tonight or any night love, I'm retired.'

'Lucky you, I'm Samantha, enjoy the show.' She blows him a kiss and moves off to serve another customer. Harry hands the drinks to Rita and Charlie and moves away from the bar.

'Blimey!' Charlie exclaims, 'How much?'

'Club prices dear boy.'

'Make it last,' Rita adds.

'I will.' Says Charlie as he takes a very small sip, 'in fact I can make it last a week.' Harry and Rita laugh as they move away from the bar to the front of the stage.

'I think you pulled there.' Rita says to Harry with a smile.

'As if,' Harry laughs, 'the words old enough, and daughter come to mind.'

'Some girls like older men.'

Harry laughs again.

'There's older and there's older, and I fall into the latter category.'

'Have you not been married Harry?' Charlie asks him, Harry moves away pretending he hasn't heard him.

'Don't go there darling.' Rita leans in to whisper in his ear, 'it's a long story and a painful one.'

'Sorry I didn't mean to….'

'No worries, I'm sure he'll tell you all about it, one day when he's ready and knows you better. Come on, let's go and join him.'

Rita sidles up beside Harry and puts her arm around his waist, he looks down at her with a half-smile. Rita smiles back but they say nothing to each other.

The band eventually hits the stage at 8.15, a quarter of an hour late but that's rock n roll for you. They play a ninety minutes set running through all the hits by The Who and more. When they leave the stage the capacity crowd is going wild for more, including Charlie. Harry watches as the boy is clapping and stamping his feet as he screams for more. Eventually the band come back and play an encore of 'Pinball Wizard' followed by the crowd pleaser 'My Generation.'

When the band finally leave the stage the three of them go back outside the club and make their way up to the promenade to cool off from the heat that was inside.

'Wow that was amazing.' Charlie said, obviously still buzzing from the music. 'I'd love to see them again.'

'They come around about every year and a half, so let's make that a date then.' Harry says as he winks at Rita who smiles back at him.

'Yeah, great.' Charlie beams with obvious excitement.

'Well if it ain't the old paedo and his bum chum.' Comes a familiar voice from behind. 'What you doing out at this time of night, trawling for some kiddies to fiddle with?'

With a huge sigh Harry turns to face Pete, who is bouncing on the balls of his feet and shrugging his shoulders with a huge grin on his face. There are three others standing behind him trying hard to look mean. Rita takes Harry's hand.

'Who is this?' She asks him.

'Nobody.'

'Nobody? You think I'm nobody?'

'You're nobody to me, just something I would scrape off my shoes.'

'Oh, really?' with the bravado he didn't have before Pete takes a step towards Harry.

'This isn't worth it Harry, come on let's go.' Charlie says to Harry whilst staring at Pete. 'You're right, he's nobody.'

'You can shut the fuck up as well, traitor, you've got the kicking of your life coming, when I've finished with paedo here.'

'I'm not sure he's going to let us just go home Charlie.'

'You're dead right there paedo.'

'Don't call him that you little child, and leave Charlie alone too.' Rita steps forward angrily. Harry puts his arm across her and pushes her back behind him.

'Looks like you've got new friends today, what happened to your last bunch of cronies?'

'Huh, they were pussies, scared of an old man; these boys aren't scared of old men.'

'You were, and they should be.' Harry gave them a 'if looks could kill' look. For just a brief second they didn't seem so sure of themselves as they had before. 'You can only be brave with a bunch of arseholes behind you.'

'Who you calling arseholes old man?' One of them shouts.

'Well, you lot if you're hanging about with the King of arseholes standing here.'

'You think I'm afraid of you?' Pete smirks, 'an old paedo, an old tart and that wimp!'

Pete moves forward quickly to hit Harry but, expecting the move, he's quicker than the boy and grabs his throat with an iron grip. The others go to move as well.

'Take another step and I'll snap the little shit's neck!' With that Harry gives them a no nonsense mean look which makes them back off. He relaxes, only very slightly, the grip on Pete's throat.'

'Get him!' Pete croaks, 'he won't do nothing.'

'Try me.' Harry increases the pressure again as he whispers to Pete. 'You've got more to lose than I have, you shouldn't call a lady you don't know, a tart.'

Harry can see two policemen about thirty yards away who are starting to take an interest in what is going on. He releases his grip on Pete's throat and pushes him away, coughing and gasping for breath as he falls to the ground.

'I told you to keep away from me, now I'm also telling you to keep away from Charlie as well. So just fuck off and don't let me see you again.'

'I'll……' Pete fights for breath, 'I'll…… I'll fucking kill you, get him you fucking idiots.' Still not sure of themselves Pete's friends start forward as if on auto pilot.

'Are these boys bothering you sir?' Harry had timed it all perfectly as the two policemen had arrived on the scene.

'Nothing I can't handle officer, thanks for asking.'

One of the officers stands over Pete.

'I'm sure I heard a threat on your life sir, from this individual here.'

'Yeah, it was kind of but I'm sure he's only jesting, aren't you Peter, just jesting?'

'Just jesting.' Pete scowls as one of his mates helps him to his feet.

'All right but I am going to need to make a report of this incident.' The officer takes out his notebook and pen. 'So if I can get all your names and addresses.'

'Happily officer.' Harry smiles and looks over to Pete to give him a wink.

The police officer takes all their details and photographs them all with his mobile phone.

'Now I expect you all to keep the peace and you,' the officer points towards Pete, 'if anything, and I mean anything should happen to this man, or this lad,' indicating Harry and Charlie. 'You will be the first one we come after, is that clear?' Pete nods reluctantly. 'Good! Now perhaps you can all make your way home, I have enough paperwork to deal with due to this already and I don't want anymore, understand?'

Everyone nods and mutters agreement, the police stand and watch as Pete and his gang leave the area.

'You sure you don't want to make a complaint Harry?' the officer asks him.

'He's just a kid who needs some sense knocking into him.'

'Please tell me you're not the one to do it.'

'Not if he keeps his distance from us I won't.'

'Be careful mate he doesn't look like the type to leave it alone and the last thing I want to do is nick you for assault, or worst.'

'It would only be self-defence Jim, self-defence.'

'You obviously know them, come on give me the full SP.'

Harry gives a deep sigh.

'He was beating the crap out of some kid the other day and I stepped in to stop him, he didn't like it very much, an old bugger like me getting the better of him.'

'What did you do?'

'Oh nothing serious, he still managed to get up and limp away.' Jim and his partner laughed.

'I don't think he's going to let it go mate.'

'Neither do I.' Harry and Jim nod knowingly at each other.

'Watch your back Harry.'

'I've got his back officer.' Charlie pipes up, Jim turns to look at him.

'That makes me feel better.' Jim adds, 'I'm counting on you.'

'Thanks Jim, I'll be seeing you, come on troops let's go home for that nightcap.'

'Goodnight Harry, Rita and, sorry forgot your name.' He looks towards Charlie.

'Charlie.'

'Yeah, goodnight Charlie.'

Pete and his gang are long gone as Harry and co make their way to the taxi rank. Rita pulls Harry close to her.

'It was him wasn't it? Charlie I mean, it was him you saved from a beating by that moron?'

'How did you guess?'

'It wasn't difficult to put two and two together, my knight in shining armour.' Rita puts her arm through Harry's and proceeds to pull him along to the taxi rank.

'Come on let's get you two home,' she says, 'I don't know about you but I really need that nightcap.'

'So do I darling, so do I. Go ahead and grab a cab Charlie, we'll limp on behind you.'

24.

Pete was angry, very angry, once again he had been shown up in front of his gang.

'You'd have had him if those coppers hadn't shown up when they did.' One of the boys, Simon, says trying to make Pete feel better about the situation.

'Fucking right I would have done.' He shouts back angrily.

'Were you afraid that he was going to strangle you?'

'Bollocks! He was never going to do that.'

'Maybe not, live to fight another day I reckon, don't you?'

'Yeah, you're right, we live to fight another day and this time I'll kill him.'

'What about the copper, he's got your address and picture?'

'Not my address he hasn't.' Pete laughs, 'don't know whose address I gave him but it ain't mine.' He laughs again.

'But he does have your picture.' His friend points out.

'So what? They won't be able to prove anything and you three will be my alibi, won't you?'

'Yeah, sure.' Dave says trying to sound convincing even if he didn't feel it.

'What are we going to do now?' Roger, the third friend asks.

'I've had enough for one night, don't care what you lot do, I'm going home.'

'Yeah me too.' Simon says and the others nod in agreement.

'Okay, I'll call you.' Pete says and stalks off without saying anything more or looking back at his three friends who stand watching him walk away.

'He's fucking dangerous.' Simon says.

'Do you think he means it, killing him I mean?' Roger asks.

'I think he means it now,' Dave adds, 'but I'm not sure if he will in the morning.'

'I do,' says Simon.

'Well I'm not going to lie for him,' says Dave, 'I won't alibi him if he kills someone.'

'He won't,' Roger says confidently 'he's all talk.'

'I hope you're right mate.' Dave says, 'anyway, I'm going home now.'

The three of them nod to each other and move off in the opposite direction to Pete.

Pete was still angry, he so much wanted to inflict some pain on the old man, but not now, he would bide his time. Right now he had no intention of going home. He desperately wanted to vent his spleen on something or someone.

He never knew his father, his mother had him when she was sixteen and never told anyone who the father was. Pete privately believed that she didn't know his identity. She constantly brought a stream of 'Uncles' who never stayed for very long. He eventually realised what they were coming for and opted to stay out of the house for as long as possible. Eventually the men stopped coming when his mother started crawling into a bottle far too much. These days she was constantly drunk, failing to notice if he was home or not.

Pete was very angry.

Despite the inclement weather, although not raining, it was very windy, he decided to take a walk up the pier to try and clear his head.

'Fucking old paedo.' He muttered to himself, looking down at his feet as he made his way along the pier, 'I'll have that piece of shit, just you wait and see.'

As he looked he saw an elderly couple with a small dog on a lead, walking towards him. As he draws up to them he grabs the woman in a head lock.

'Gimme your money granddad or I'll snap her neck.' He shouts at the man.

'Don't, don't hurt her.' The man says as he fumbles with his wallet to hand over the few pounds that he has in there. 'We're only pensioners, this is all I've got.'

Pete looks at the fifteen pounds the old man holds out to him with shaky hands and let's go of his wife who clutches her chest.

'Is that it?' Pete shouts.

'We're just pensioners, like I said.'

'Don! Don! I think I'm having a heart attack.' The woman falls to her knees and her husband rushes over to her.

'You little shit, you've given her a heart attack, call an ambulance.'

Pete panics, shoves the money into his pocket then turns and runs back down the pier.

'Help me!' The old man shouts, his cries ringing in Pete's ears as he runs away.

25.

Sunday morning, the day after the Who's Who show, Harry is up early. Knowing he's likely to get greasy and dirty he dresses in some old clothes without taking a shower. Before doing anything else he makes a large mug of tea and a couple of slices of toast.

After the clash with Pete and co they had hopped a cab and came back to Harry's for that much needed nightcap. Charlie had a can of lager, as Harry promised him, whist he and Rita had a couple of large whiskies. For a while they discussed the show, which had really impressed Charlie, who wanted to know more about the real Who. He vowed to go and check them out on YouTube and maybe get some CDS when he had some cash. Harry promised to pay him for helping with the scooter.

The incident with Pete wasn't mentioned.

Charlie eventually went home, promising to come back in the morning to help strip and rebuild the scooter with the new parts they'd brought from Ed's daughter. Rita stayed for one more whiskey but eventually, as it was quite late, took a cab home.

By the time Harry had finished his tea and toast it was approaching nine o'clock. Charlie had promised to be there at around that time. As Harry was considering making another cup of tea the doorbell rang, he was impressed that Charlie made it on time and went to let him in.

'On time mate, well done.' said Harry as he let him into the house. 'Any problems with your dad last night?'

'No, he was satisfied I was with you and Rita, anyway, I wasn't that late.'

'No sign of your friend and mine either?'

'No, but I'm sure we haven't seen the last of him. Police or no police you've shown him up twice now and he's not the sort to turn his back on that.'

'Hmm,' Harry looks thoughtful and makes his way back to the kitchen. 'Cup of tea?'

'Please. What are you going to do about him?'

'I'll cross that bridge when I get to it, I've met his type more than once in the past.' Once more he absentmindedly touches the scar on his face. 'It didn't always go well for me either.'

'Your scar you mean?' Charlie is aware of Harry touching it. 'Are you going to tell me how you got it?'

'One day but this isn't it, we've got work to do, but first, tea.'

With that Harry boils another kettle and this time makes a pot of tea. With mugs in hand they make their way into the garage where they first take out every scooter part from the boxes brought from Denise's house. The most important being the engine which they urgently needed to replace.

'Right young Charles, you can either strip down the new engine and check it out or remove the old one.'

'I'll strip the new one.'

'Okey dokey, you'll find all the tools you need over there in that box as well, as rags and oil. Upwards and onwards.'

Harry goes to the portable CD player and puts on 'Who's Next', Charlie smiles and gets to work. While he strips the new engine, Harry removes the old one plus the carburettor which he also intended to replace.

Four hours and a few more CDS later Charlie had stripped, cleaned and rebuilt the engine ready for it to be replaced in the scooter. Harry declared a break and called for a pizza delivery. He'd made sure the fridge was stocked with a sufficient quantity of quality lager for Charlie, and Guinness for himself. When the pizza was all gone they returned to the task in hand which was getting closer to the rebuilding.

After a few minor setbacks, like the fuel pipe being too rotten to put back and Harry having to go and get a new one, they were almost finished when Rita arrived.

'Not too late am I?' She asked.

'Almost, just in time. Did you close up early to be here?'

'No, the ever wonderfully loyal Sara said she'd close up for me, again.'

'About time you gave that girl a raise.'

'What? She's already earning a small fortune, what with tips and all.' Harry laughs.

'Charlie here is putting the finishing touches to the engine before we attempt to start her up.' Harry is beaming from ear to ear, Rita comes up beside him to put her arm through his.

'You look so…, so alive Harry, more alive than I've seen you in a long time.' He turns to her and smiles.

'I couldn't have done it without him', he says nodding towards Charlie who, having put oil in the engine, had finished at last and was wiping the grease from his hands. 'So what do you think?' he says to Charlie.

'What do I think? I think it looks like the dogs bollocks, that's what I think.'

'Oi! Watch your language, ladies present.' Rita laughs and playfully punches Harry on the arm. 'You say it's the poodle's parts.' Charlie gives him a questioning look. 'The dog's bollocks, fool.'

'Oi! Watch your language, ladies present.' Charlie replies and they all laugh together.

'He's right though,' Rita remarks, 'it does look bloody good.'

'Yea……………h, scrubbed up well it has.' Harry quips in an imitation of Yoda from Star Wars.

'So are you going to give it go?' Charlie asks.

'Yeah, but maybe later.'

'What do you mean?' Charlie looks upset, Rita also gives Harry a strange look.

'I thinks someone else deserves the first attempt to start her up, don't you Reet?'

Rita catches on.

'Yes, yes I do.' They both look in Charlie's direction.

'What?' they just look at him for a few seconds until………..
'You mean………….?'

'He's twigged.' Harry says to Rita.

94

'He's twigged.' Harry replies.

'Seriously?'

'If you can get it started you can be the first one to have a ride, but not on the road, you haven't got a licence yet. You can get one when you are sixteen, you don't need to pass any test to ride this but I'll help you learn, if you want.'

'Do I? You bet I do.'

'So it's not wimpy anymore to ride a scooter?'

Charlie just laughs and turns towards the machine where he bleeds some fuel into the carburettor then flicks the switch to start.

'Ready?' Charlie says to Harry.

'Ready.'

Charlie straddles the scooter and kicks down on the starter, the engine coughs a couple of times and dies. Harry raises his eyebrows and nods as if to say 'do it again.' Charlie kicks down, the engine coughs again but this time he remembers to open the throttle a little bit more and it kicks into life. They all laugh, Rita jumps up and down clapping her hands while Harry goes over to slap Charlie on the back. He slowly opens up the throttle a bit more as the engine starts to purr beautifully then eases it back down to tick over on it's own.

'Beautiful Charlie, absolutely beautiful. Now all we have to do is fix the panels back and she's almost ready for a test run.'

'Almost?' Charlie questions.

'Yes, almost, sadly it has to be insured and taxed but it can't have that without an MOT certificate.' Rita says putting a bit of a dampener on the mood.

'That's true and I don't have the money to do that at the moment do I Reet' Harry looks pleadingly at Rita.

'I told you I would sort that out for you didn't I?' She replied with a smile on her face as she opens up her handbag to remove an envelope which she hands to Harry. He opens it up and a huge smile spreads across his face making him go over to put his arm around her shoulders and plant a peck on her cheek.

'You're too good to me Reet.'

'I know, so you have the insurance cover note, take it in tomorrow for an MOT then I can get the tax for you.'

'Thanks darling, okay I think it's time for a celebratory beer.'

26.

'I don't like Mondays.' Terry muttered to himself as he opened his workshop doors then burst into song. 'The silicon chip inside of her, gets switched to overload, dum, dum, dum, dum I don't like Mondays, tell me why, dum, dum I want to shoo ooo ooo oot the whole day down. Yeah Bob, so do I mate.'

Once through the door he switches on the light to glance around at the place he'd been coming to for nearly all of his working life. It was all looking a bit tired, but then so was Terry. He thought to himself, time to retire. He had wanted to pass it on to his grandson but he didn't seem to have any interest in motor mechanics so he was considering putting it up for sale. After all he owned the freehold. The forecourt had closed years ago, as they couldn't compete with the supermarkets on petrol prices.

When the forecourt first closed Terry started selling new and second hand bikes but had run that down in recent years. The machine he'd sold the week before would be his last. With just a couple of second hand ones left, those he was passing on to another dealer then that would be the end of it. However there was just one that needed an MOT and that was the main reason he'd come to the workshop on a Monday morning. He'd checked it over himself at the weekend and if he still did MOT testing, he would have passed it.

After parking his own bike inside Terry wheeled the other one out onto the road and locked the workshop doors again.

It was only a short trip to the MOT station and Terry made it in just over ten minutes, without breaking the speed limit he thought to himself. There would have been a time when the speed limit wouldn't have meant a thing to him, but that was after a couple of bans for speeding. A lesson well learnt, eventually. On arrival mechanic Dave was waiting for him.

'Morning Tel', want a cuppa first or are you in a hurry?' Dave asked indicating the kettle in his hand.

'Cuppa sounds like a wonderful idea.' Dave nods and goes into his office to switch the kettle on, Terry follows him. 'Are you busy today?'

'Got a few MOTS booked in, some services, and an oil change, enough to keep us going for the day. How about you?'

'Just this, I'm winding down, time to retire so I'm going to sell the workshop. I don't expect anyone will take it on as a business, more likely to interest a property developer who would pull it down and build flats there.'

'I might know someone who'd be interested, that's quite a bit of real estate you've got there, must be worth a bob or two.'

'I hope so, I'm considering buying something in Spain. I'm fed up with the British climate and starting to get arthritis in my hands which isn't helped by it. I need to be somewhere warm.'

'I'll give him a call later and let you know.'

'Thanks Dave, I apprecia......' Terry stops mid-sentence, 'I don't fucking believe it.'

'What?' Terry points at Harry who pulls up outside.

'Look, do me favour, tell him out there with the scooter to come back in an hour, you're too busy at the moment.'

'Well that's no less than the truth.' Dave leaves the office and approaches Harry, Terry ducks down below the window.

'I don't believe it.' He mutters to himself. 'I don't see him for years and then twice in just a few days.'

Dave comes back in and laughs at Terry crouching on the floor.

'Problem is there?'

'No, well, yes we've got history but it was years ago. I haven't seen him in yonks and then he pops up last week, he didn't see me then either.' Terry gets back up to sit in the office chair.

'So, would it be spanners at twenty paces?'

'Yeah, maybe.'

'Well I better get your bike done so you get the hell out of Dodge, maybe it will be yonks before you see him again.'

'Maybe, I'm getting too old for all that stuff.' Dave smiles and goes back out to work on Terry's bike.

After a half hour the MOT is finished and Terry is well away before Harry returns.

27.

Harry rode back on his newly MOT'd scooter, all it needed now was road tax, which he promptly bought from the main post office in the city centre, with the cash Rita had lent him. After fixing the disc to the holder he stood back to look at it. It had been many years since his pride and joy had been on the road let alone looking as sparkling as it was now. Feeling almost as excited as he had when he first bought it Harry decided to take it round to show Rita, who was only a few blocks away.

He pulled up in the back yard of the café and went in through the back door which led into the kitchen. Both Rita and Sara were serving customers of which there were quite a few. They were both pleased to see him.

'Help yourself to coffee, as you can see we're a bit rushed off our feet.' Rita called to him, 'If you want to eat you'll have to wait.'

'No its ok, a coffee will do. I've just got the beastie taxed.'

'Terrific,' Sara said, 'Can I have a look?'

'Sure, as soon as you've got a moment.' Harry made himself a coffee and sat down behind the counter. It wasn't long before all the customers had their orders so Rita and Sara could relax for a few moments. This enabled Sara to come out to have a look at the scooter.

'That's impressive Harry, when you going to take me for a ride?'

'Anytime you like, but I have promised the first ride to someone else.'

'Would that be Charlie?' Harry looked surprised.

'You've heard about Charlie then?'

'Yes Rita filled me in on Saturday night's gig, including your brush with some of Brighton's louts.'

'Harry!' Rita calls out to him from the kitchen, 'Ritchie Taylor is on the phone looking for you.'

'Coming!' He replies and goes back into the café to take the call. 'Hi Ritchie.'

'Harry, when I couldn't reach you at home I thought you might be in the café.'

'Only just got here mate, good timing.'

'I've spoken to the ex Mrs Conrad who, after I persuaded her that you were a good bloke, agreed to let me give you her mobile number.'

'Does she know it's about her son?'

'Yes she does.'

'Okay, hang on a sec while I get something to write on,' Rita passes him her note pad and pen, Harry gives her a quick smile of thanks. 'Right, hit me with it.' He quickly takes down the number. 'Thanks for that Ritchie, how did she sound?'

'A bit wary at first but when I personally vouched for you she seemed to relax. Let me know how you get on.'

'Will do, and thanks again.'

'Is that the number for Charlie's mother?'

'Yes it is, do you mind if I call her now?'

'No I don't, but maybe I should speak to her first to put her mind at rest, suggest I come with you to see her. What do you think?' Rita says as she puts her hand on Harry's while he still has his on the phone.

'Do you mind?'

'No, of course not, Charlie seems a nice lad to me and if there's a chance of reuniting him with his mother I would love to help.' Harry smiles and hands the number to Rita.

'You're one in a million Reet.'

'I know I am, now give me the phone.' Harry passes the phone and she dials the number, 'What's her name?'

'Christine Conrad.' Rita holds her finger up for Harry to be quiet as someone answers after only two rings.

'Hello, my name is Rita Hanson and I'm looking for Christine Conrad, can you help?' There's a moments silence at the other end.

'That's me but I haven't been Christine Conrad for over a year now, I've gone back to my maiden name of DeVoy, how did you get my number?'

'I'm ringing of behalf of Harry York who was given your number by Chief Inspector Taylor of Brighton CID, I believe he spoke to you about Harry.'

'Yes, that's right, he said it was something to do with my son Charlie?'

'Yes, it is, Charlie has become very friendly with Harry and myself and we'd like to come and talk to you about him.'

'Does Charlie know you have this number, have you given it to him as well?'

'No, no we wouldn't do that without your permission. We'd like to come and talk to you first.'

'Does my husband, well my ex-husband, know about this?'

'Of course not, it's only Charlie's welfare we are interested in, certainly not your husbands, oh and yours of course.'

'Well, all right, I don't go to Brighton, ever so....'

'No problem we can come to you, you're not in Scotland are you?'

'No only Portslade, not so far. When would you like to come?'

'Hang on, let me check with Harry.' Rita puts her hand over the mouthpiece and whispers to him, 'When can you go?'

'Tomorrow, if it's good for you.' Rita nods and goes back to the phone.

'How's tomorrow, in the evening as I'm working till six. We can come straight after, be with you about seven?'

'That would be okay, do you have something to write down my address?'

'Yes, go on.'

'Inspector Taylor said I can trust Harry, please tell me I can, and you won't give my number or address to anyone else.' Christine sounds desperate on the other end of the line.

'Trust me Christine,'

'Chrissie, please call me Chrissie, my few friends do.'

'Chrissie, you can trust us both, Harry and I have known each other forever and I would trust him with my life.' Chrissie goes on to give Rita her details after which they say their farewells then Rita hangs up and turns to Harry. 'She can trust us can't she Harry?'

'You need to ask? Really? You know I'm only interested in reuniting Charlie with his mother.'

'Of course you are, I'm sorry. I don't know what I was thinking maybe it's just, oh I don't know. It's just she sounded so, so sad and wary of trusting us.'

'She gave you her address didn't she?'

'Well yes, I hope it's her address, it could be anywhere.'

'No. I'm sure it's right, I think she wants to make contact with her son and we are the best way she can do it.'

'So tomorrow,'

'Tomorrow it is.'

'I'm going to start keeping a log of all the petrol you owe me.'

''No worries, one of my pensions are due to kick in soon so I'll spot you some cash and........' Rita puts her hand on his.

'Don't be silly, I'm joking, I like Charlie too and this visit to his mother is very important so I'm sure I can spare a couple of gallons of jungle juice.'

Harry smiles and gently touches her cheek.

'Thanks, I really appreciate it.'

27.

The next day it's still raining, not hard but enough to make it miserable to be out in. Harry didn't feel like riding the scooter down to the café so he forked out for a taxi which dropped him off on the promenade. He just wanted to look out at the blackness that hung over the sea. The lights on the pier illuminated a number of people enjoying the facilities. After taking a deep breath Harry took the twenty or so steps to the café which was now showing the closed sign despite having two people sitting nursing a couple of coffees.

The door was locked forcing Harry to tap on it to attract Rita's attention. She opens the door with a smile, and lets him in.

'Would you like a quick coffee? These people are nearly finished but we have time anyway.'

'No. it's all right, I'd rather be a day early than five minutes late.'

The couple finish their coffees, say their thanks and farewells then leave. Sara had already gone home, all the clearing up had been done before Harry arrived. All Rita had to do was wash the cups the last customers had used and put on her coat.

'Ready?' She asks Harry.

'Ready as I'll ever be.' He replies.

Rita locks the front door then they make their way out the back to her car.

'What are you going to say to her?' Harry asks as Rita turns out of the café's back yard onto the street.

'What am I going to say?' Rita asks with a surprised tone. 'I'm just the taxi driver along for the ride.'

'You'll be better at this than me, you're a woman.'

'Oh you noticed! So how does that make me better qualified to speak to her?'

'I think you will be able to put her at ease, maybe not jump in straight away talking about Charlie. Get her to talk about the situation, what happened with her husband and why she ran off without her son.'

'See, you do know how to deal with her. Right, I'll try to put her at ease, show her we're not devils in disguise. Look don't worry, we'll play it by ear.'

'Easy for you to say.' Rita gives him a thoughtful glance and turns on to the A27 which is pretty busy with traffic. Harry looks out the window and retreats into his own thoughts, wondering if he is doing the right thing.

Rita is thinking the same.

28.

The woman who answered the door was not what Harry had been expecting. The vision he had in his mind was of a short, slightly overweight mousey woman with short hair and a nervous disposition. She was definitely nervous, but that was where his expectations ended. Christine DeVoy was a slim, attractive dark haired lady standing about an inch taller than Harry's five foot nine, and probably in her early forties.

'Mister York I presume and this must be Ms Hanson, please come in out of the cold.'

'Thank you,' Harry stepped aside to allow Rita to go before him. They followed Chrissie into the lounge where there was another woman, about the same age as her, and a man marginally older than Harry.'

'This is my sister Sandra and my father George.'

'We're very pleased to meet you all,' Harry puts out his hand to shake theirs, 'I'm Harry York and this is my, er, friend Rita Hanson.' Rita shakes hands with them as well.

'Please sit down,' Chrissie points to the sofa for Harry and Rita to sit on. 'Can I get you a drink, tea, coffee, something stronger?'

'No we're fine thank you, a bit apprehensive but otherwise fine.' Rita answers.

'You're apprehensive, how about me?' Chrissie wrings her hands nervously. 'I don't know you people.'

'No, you don't.' Harry interjects, 'but, hopefully, my old friend DCI Ritchie Taylor gave me a glowing testimonial.'

'Well, yes he did.'

'He's known me since he was a rookie copper so I hope that counts for something, after all, you've invited us into your home.'

'Yes Mister York, my daughter has extended her trust to you but we are all curious to know your relationship with my grandson.'

'Please call me Harry, can I ask, when was the last time you saw your grandson Mr DeVoy?'

'Over a year ago now.'

'And why is that?'

'I don't think it's your place to be asking me questions do you?' George makes a prickly reply.

'Okay, I understand, so to answer your question I first came across Charlie when I rescued him from being beaten up by a gang of youths.' The three relatives look at each other without speaking. 'I cleaned him up and sent him home. Since then he's been helping me rebuild my scooter. He's a good lad but he seems to think that you, Chrissie, left him and his father, for another man.'

'What!! That's not true, who told him that? Of course, his bloody father, the fucking bastard!'

'Now Chrissie, no need for that language.' George says whilst looking sternly at her.

'No need? After what he did to me I think I was being vey controlled.'

'What did he do to you then?' Rita asks her.

'I suffered years of beatings, humiliations and rape, you name it, he did it.'

'Charlie has never mentioned seeing any of that?'

'Oh no the bastard was clever, never my face, always somewhere it didn't show. Broken ribs from him kicking me with steel toe-caped boots, cigarette burns on my tits.' Chrissie starts to choke back tears with the memory. Rita reaches out to take her hand while Sandra puts a comforting arm around her shoulders. Suddenly Chrissie loses control and bursts into tears.

'He would come home drunk,' Sandra adds 'and force her to have sex with him, not gentle, loving sex but brutal rape. The man's an animal.'

'Why didn't you go to the police?' Harrys asks her.

'I did, eventually, but they don't like getting into domestic disputes. The officers who came to see me said I could press charges but any kind of assault, especially rape, was difficult to prove in a marriage situation. I just didn't want to put Charlie through the exposure, press and all that goes with it. So they put me in touch with a woman's shelter which is where I went at first.'

'Why didn't you take Charlie with you?' Rita asked her.

'David said he'd kill me if I took Charlie, he didn't care if I left but he wasn't going to let me take his son, and I believe he wouldn't think twice about doing it.'

Everything went quiet for a few moments, Rita and Harry were trying to digest what Chrissie had told them.

'I'm sorry Chrissie,' Rita finally speaks up, 'that all sounds truly horrific but death threat or no death threat nothing would have stopped me from taking my son.'

'Do you have kids Rita?'

'Er no,' Rita pauses and looks at Harry for a second. 'No I don't but if I did I know what I would have done. Look I'm sorry I'm not passing judgment on you, we're all different after all.'

'You have to understand, I had been beaten, mentally as well as physically, I was in no position to take my son let alone look after him.'

'My sister has been in therapy ever since, my father pays the rent on this flat, such as it is. There is a small second bedroom, of course we are hoping that Charlie will come here one day.'

'All right, trust me, I truly understand how bad this must have been for you. Harry leans forward and takes her hand. 'But I'm really concerned about Charlie, I'm not sure if his father is hitting him but the boy is quite obviously not happy. Like I said before he thinks you left him for another man, how do you think that makes him feel? So back to my earlier question George, when was the last time you saw your Grandson?'

George now looks sheepish.

'I don't know, before Chrissie left Brian.'

'Don't you all think he deserves to know the truth?'

'Yes, perhaps you're right.' Chrissie answers.

'Why do you care?' George asks Harry.

'Because I see a little bit of me in him. He still thinks these yobs who beat the crap out of him are his mates. If he continues to hang out with them he's going to end in trouble and maybe even doing some jail time. He hasn't got a loving home life which is why he's spending time with this gang. He's recently been spending time with Rita and myself, as I said helping with the scooter and we took him to a concert last weekend. It's kept him away from them but we're not his parents, there's only so much we can do. We're all right for the moment but he really needs his mother.'

'Can you not have him live with you?' Rita asks

'Are you sure he wants to?' Chrissie asks with a pleading look on her face. 'I mean he thinks I left him for another man.'

'I'm sure of it, especially when he knows the truth of the situation.' Harry adds.

'What do you think dad?' Chrissie looks around at George.

'I don't think there's any question love, bring him here first then we can sort out something better for the two of you.'

'I presume you're not divorced yet?' Rita asks. Chrissie shakes her head. 'Then get him here, file for divorce and get custody.'

'Does he know you're here?'

'God no.' Harry jumps in, 'I didn't want to get his hopes up before I spoke to you, after all you might not have been interested in making contact.'

'I am, we are but what about Brian? I still think he would carry out his threat.'

'You leave him to me.' Harry replied, 'there is no way I will let him hurt either of you.'

'Don't do anything that will get you into trouble, I wouldn't want that to happen on my behalf.' Chrissie says with a pleading tone to her voice.

'Don't worry,' Rita says, 'Harry knows how to deal with bullies without getting physical.'

Harry doesn't say anything.

'I'll be so grateful if you can bring my Charlie back to me.'

'We will Chrissie, I promise.' Harry says softly.

'I think this calls for a drink.' George says as he stands up, 'a glass of wine everyone?'

'That would be nice, thank you.' Harry says.

'Just a small one for me, I'm driving.' Says Rita.

George fetches a bottle of Chardonnay and pours everyone a glass.

'Here's to Charlie.' Rita says as she lifts her glass.

'Charlie!' Everyone says together.

29.

'Do you think we're doing the right thing?' Rita asks Harry as they drive back to his house.

'I hope so, well, yes of course I think it's the right thing, I meant what I said, I think we should get him away from his father and this gang. I know it will all end in tears if we don't and I'm sure Charlie wants to be with his mother.'

'How are you going to handle it, will you just tell him you've seen his mother and she wants him to come and live with her?'

'No, just let me think about it for a few days, there's no hurry, I mean it's been over a year since he's seen her, another few days won't hurt. I'd also welcome any suggestions or ideas from you.'

'I'm sure I can think of something.' They slip into contemplated silence for the rest of the journey back to Harry's house, where Rita drops him off.

Harry leans back in the car.

'Coming in to have one for the road?'

'No, I need to get home I'm behind on my paper work,' Harry gives her a sad look. 'No, it's not just a line, I'm tired and I have to get this done.'

'No worries,' Harry smiles 'I'm thinking of taking Charlie up to the Downs in the next couple of days to let him have a ride on the scooter. We can't do it on the road at the moment, he hasn't got a licence and can't get one until he's sixteen. I was thinking maybe you could come along as well and we can discuss the situation with his mother then. We could probably have some kind of game plan by then, when do you think?'

Rita sighs.

'You have a way of asking that I find really difficult to say no to.' She laughs as Harry breaks into a wide grin.

'Really? In that case….'

'However there are some things I find easy.' They both laugh, then Harry blows her a goodnight kiss, closes the door and watches as she drives away. By now it is getting quite late and he goes inside to find a beer in the fridge before switching on the TV to watch nothing in particular. He's not really taking notice of what is on but contemplating how to approach Charlie when a bottle smashes against his front door.

After his last encounter with Pete, Harry had placed his old baseball bat by the front door. He casually opens the door with his hand placed on the bat that couldn't be seen by anyone outside. Within a fraction of a second another bottle smashes against the wall just inches from his head. Pete and two of his mates are standing at the end of the path, grinning and jeering.

'Careful you old paedo, we don't want you shitting your pants there now do we?' The three boys laugh loudly.

'Why am I not surprised to see you?' Harry says with a note of resignation in his voice then picks up the bat to stride purposefully down the path towards them.

'Another new bunch of goons I see.'

'You think you scare me old man?' Pete stands with his feet apart in an attempt to show bravado, Harry however is unflinching as he whirls the bat in the air to slap it into his palm.

'Yes, I think I do, after all I've got this,' he slaps the bat in his palm a couple more times, 'and I've still got your knife.' With that Harry makes a feint towards Pete who flinches back. 'What are you doing here? I told you to keep away.'

Pete flexes his shoulders in an attempt to show that he isn't scared.

'I want to show that I'm not scared of you.'

Harry leans in closer to whisper in his ear.

'Oh but you are, otherwise you wouldn't need these two goons to back you up.' He points the bat at the other two boys without taking his eyes away from Pete's. 'I can smell the fear on you. You want to believe I'm some old man but you know that's really not the case.'

'Do him Pete!' One of the other boys tries to egg him on, Harry waves the bat at them, still without taking his eyes from Pete's

'You're afraid because you don't know how far I'll go. You thought I was some push over but trust me, you'll never go as far as I will.'

Suddenly his left hand shoots out to grab the boy by the throat. One of the other two makes to come forward but Harry shoots him a look with the bat that freezes the boy to the spot. The other one stands his ground looking unsure of what to do. Pete starts panicking as he chokes and gags, Harry releases his grip slightly and Pete gasps for air.

'Maybe you think the three of you can take me. Well maybe you can but I can assure you I'll crack your head open so wide first I'll be able to see that pea brain you've got in there.'

With that Harry let's go of his throat leaving him to fall to the ground still gasping and coughing. He looks over to his cohorts who are backing away before turning to run off down the road leaving Pete alone and on his knees.

'Some friends you have there.'

'This isn't over!' Pete starts crying, 'this isn't fucking over! I'll.....I'll.'

Harry leans down and places the bat under the boys chin to gently lift his face up.

'Really? Right now I could call the police and get them to charge you with, oh let me see. Assault on another boy, damage to my property, attempted murder with your knife that is safe in a plastic bag with your fingerprints all over. Threatening behaviour, witnessed by two police officers, how about all that for starters? What do you think the courts will see, a helpless kid or a helpless old man being terrorised by some young thug?'

'It's not over.' Pete mutters.

'It had fucking better be, you really don't want to mess with me, shit for brains, now fuck off before I change my mind and run you in to the police.'

Harry pushes Pete back with the bat and turns round to walk back to his house swinging the bat at his side. He then lifts it up onto his shoulder whilst whistling and goes inside to close the door without looking back.

Once inside the house he leans back on the door and takes a deep breath.

'I'm getting to old for this shit, I need a fucking drink!'

****

'Sara has certainly been earning her wages these past few weeks while I'm running around with you. I had to get a part timer to come in and help her, I'll be looking to you for a contribution.'

Rita, Harry and Charlie are standing by Rita's car on the South Downs just outside Brighton. For the first time in quite a while there is a clear blue sky with the sun shining high in the sky. Although January had turned into February it was still cold, but dry.

Rita had brought Charlie in her car while Harry had ridden there on his scooter. Charlie was looking dapper in a smart suit with a long Parka covering it, Harry is just dressed in jeans and a denim jacket.

'You're looking sharp today.' Harry says turning his palms up towards Charlie, 'where'd you get the suit?'

'I've had it a while and dad gave me some money for the Parka, picked it up in the Lanes.'

'Well you look every inch a Mod mate, I'm proud of you. So, what about it?' Harry cranes his head to the right where the scooter stands.

'It's weird, I always thought that riding a scooter was a bit, I dunno.'

'Wimpy?' Charlie laughs.

'Yeah, that's what I said, didn't I?'

'It's not about what you ride Charlie, it's about who you are.'

'And who am I?'

'That's the beauty of it all, you are whoever you want to be, the world is yours now, not an old fart like me.'

'You're not an old fart, you're a great, strong guy, I wish I could be more like you.'

'You can be, but I'll tell you what you're not. You're not the same boy I rescued from a beating and you're certainly not like the brain dead thugs that were doing the beating.'

'Harry's right, you're a good kid, no sorry, a good young man.'

'You've got a talent with engines, maybe you should look at getting some kind of apprenticeship.'

'I wouldn't know where to start.'

'You just leave that to me, I've got a few ideas, if you'd be interested that is.' Harry muses,

'Dead right I'd be interested.'

'Okay, now are you going keep waffling or are you going to ride that thing?'

'I'm going to ride.' Charlie replies and Harry smiles, Charlie does too.

'Right, take it easy to start with, you're not in a race and we don't need you stacking it up after all the time and work we've spent on it, now do we?'

'I'll be careful Harry, don't worry.'

With that Charlie kicks the engine into life and revs the throttle while shooting Harry and Rita a beaming smile. Harry nods approval as Charlie guns the engine and takes off just a little bit faster than Harry would have liked.

'Woo hoo!' Charlie cries out as he speeds away laughing and loving the moment. He keeps going until he becomes a spot in the distance to Harry and Rita.

'Do you think he's planning on coming back?' Rita whispers an aside.

'He will,' Harry laughs, 'if he knows what's good for him.' They laugh together then suddenly realise the car radio is playing and old track by The Kinks. Harry opens the door and leans in to turn it up very loud.

'That's' an oldie.' Rita observes.

'Girl, you really got me going' Harry starts to sing 'you got me so I don't know what I'm doing.'

'The oldies are the best.' Rita smiles.

'You sure?'

'Absolutely.'

'What about Justin Bieber or One Direction?'

'Oh gimme a break!' Rita slaps Harry playfully on the arm. 'Well, some of the new stuff is fine, some of it you can even tap your feet or dance to. But nothing beats a good classic, and I love a good classic.' With that she takes his hands. 'Let's dance.'

Harry and Rita start to jive along to the Kinks track that fades into another one which they keep dancing to. They are so wrapped up in the dance that they don't notice Charlie coming back until he pulls up beside them. The aura around him is electric.

'How was that?' Harry asks him.

'A-fucking-mazing!'

'Hey mind the language, ladies present.' Harry says, Rita laughs.

'Oh Harry I've heard you use that and worse over the years.' Rita laughs, Harry laughs too.

'Who me? Never.' He continues to laugh as he looks at his watch. 'I think we need to make a move if we're going to get there on time.'

'Get where?'

'Back into town, to Madeira Drive in fact, to meet the lads.'

'The lads?' Charlie looks puzzled and looks over to Rita for an explanation but she just smiles.

'Yeeeah, the lads, come on saddle up, you can ride pillion this time, and we'll follow Rita.'

Charlie just shakes his head in confusion, dons his crash helmet and climbs onto the scooter.

30.

The weather on the seafront is perfect, cold but sunny with a reasonably calm sea. The three of them are leaning against Rita's car eating an ice cream recently bought from the van not far from the pier. They are not speaking, each one of them lost in their private thoughts. Harry is still contemplating how to tackle the subject of Charlie's mother with the boy, while Rita is wondering when he is actually going to do it. Charlie is still buzzing from the ride he had on the Downs and the trip back to town.

Suddenly Harry can hear the feint sound of scooter engines which quickly start to get louder.

'Here they come!' He says with a mouthful of ice-cream.

'The lads?' Charlie asks.

'The lads.' Harry replies.

Less than a minute later three scooters turn into the drive from the roundabout, waving and honking their horns as they come towards them to eventually pull up.

'Well who's this here, looks like Action Man?' Frank laughs as he takes off his helmet.

'Action Man?' Asks Charlie.

'Before your time matey. So you must be Charlie.' Steve quips.

'Yeah, that's me.'

'Well we're pleased to meet you Charlie.' Bernie puts his hand out to shake Charlie's, 'Harry's told us all about you.'

'All good I hope.'

'Oh no, nothing but bad.' Bernie replies.

A few day trippers pass by to make some comments about the scooters and take some photographs. The lads strike some poses for them as well as bringing Charlie into the fold.

'Having fun mate?' Steve asks him.

'Yes, one of the best days I've had for ages.'

'Better than knocking around with that old mob of yours isn't it?' Harry asks him.

'Yes, it certainly is. Is it all right if I sit on the bi….. Sorry, scooter for a bit?'

'Of course, you've earned the right.'

'I'll have to get one of my own one day.'

'You never know what's around the corner.'

'I'll have to start saving. Well I'll have to get a job first, a Saturday job at least, until I've finished school that is.'

'Good idea.'

'Hey Harry,' Steve calls out, 'do you remember the first time we all came down here together?'

'Do I?' Harry leans back on Rita's car and touches the scar on his face. 'How could I forget?'

31.

Harry can feel the tip of the Rockers finger pressing into his chest whilst smelling the mixture of smoke and beer on his breath. He narrows his eyes and pushes back on the finger with his body.

'Fuck your breath stinks.' Harry sneers.

'Why don't you Mod bastards get back on those fucking hair dryers and piss off home?

Harry can feel the hairs on the back of his neck stand up with anger, just like the hackles on a dog.

'You should choose your words carefully.' Harry says with a grimace.

'Me? You started with the insults.'

'Come on Harry', Ed's voice comes from behind, 'let's go back the other way, this isn't worth it.'

'Oh no, it's not as easy as that.' The Rocker adds, 'We were here first and we've been insulted.'

'Look we don't want any trouble we're just here to enjoy the sights and have a couple of beers before we go home.' Ed continues.

'Well, looks like you just might have to fight your way out of town.'

Ed looks as if he might cut and run but a warning glance from Steve puts a stop to any ideas in that direction. Before Ed can reconsider his position, Harry head butts the Rocker in front of him, who goes down like a pack of cards. In a flash the other Rockers are upon them with fists flying. It only takes a few seconds for the one Harry attacked to get back to his feet, nose bleeding, to take a swing as his attacker.

'You fucking little shit!' he screams at Harry as he manages to dodge the punch. 'I'll fucking kill you for that!' As he screams the threat at Harry he pulls a flick knife out of his leather jacket and flashes the blade towards him.

Ed looks horrified.

'He's got a knife,' he shouts. 'Leg it!'

Terry lunges forward with the knife.

Yes, Harry remembered that day, very well.

32

Meanwhile, on the other side of town, as the boys are enjoying the day with Charlie, Terry is servicing his motorbike whilst listening to Gene Vincent on his sound system and singing along with 'Pistol Packing Mama'. Coincidentally, Terry was also thinking about that summer's day when he first came face to face with Harry York.

And how it change both lives.

'Terry!' a voice from the doorway lifted him out of his thoughts. It was Andy, his part time helper. 'There's someone here to see you.'

'If it's a complaint tell them the owner's out and I'm not interested.'

'I don't think it's a complaint, he says he's your grandson.'

'All right,' Terry heaves a sigh, 'you'd better show him in.'

Pete comes through the door with his head hanging low and a sheepish look on his face.'

'Peter, come on in, you're looking a little less than pleased with yourself, what's wrong?'

Pete was in fact Terry's grandson by his eldest daughter Lynn, who had managed to get herself pregnant when she was sixteen. Having refused to name the father Terry was unable to go and deal with him in the way he would have liked. Lynn refused to have an abortion so Terry and his wife agreed to look after her and the baby. That is until she met the man she eventually married when Pete was eight. The marriage lasted less than a year and she became an alcoholic leaving Pete to spend as much time away from the house as possible.

'There's some old geezer who keeps threatening me.'

Terry puts down the spanner he was using to wipe his hands on a nearby rag. He stands up to lean back against his bike, still wiping his hands.

'Oh yeah and what is he threatening to do?'

'The other day he grabbed me by the throat and almost choked me to death.'

'And he did this why?'

'I don't know, I was just standing in the street near his house with some of my mates and he came out shouting and swearing at us. Before I could do anything or move away he was grabbing me, I thought he was going to kill me.'

'Well I think that sounds highly unlikely, are you sure you didn't do something else to make him angry?'

'No, honest.'

'Who is this old man and how old is he?'

'I think he might be called Harry, about your age I would say.'

'Harry eh, about my age and you think that's old?'

'I didn't mean you're old, just...oh you know what I mean.' Terry laughs.

'Don't worry boy, I know I'm old. What does he look like?'

'Longish grey hair, bit of a beard but maybe he just doesn't shave every day, a bit taller than me.'

'Sounds like a lot of men my age.'

'Oh and he has a scar running from his eye to his ear.'

With that Terry raises his eyebrows.

'A scar you say?'

'Yeah, do you know him?'

'I think I might boy, I think I might. If it's who I think it is we have history, but he's not the sort to pick on a kid like you. What are you not telling me?'

'Nothing grandad, honest.'

'All right, I believe you, I think. How far away from you does he live?'

'A few streets away.'

'Right, I want you to promise me you'll keep well away from him, don't go near his house, don't even walk down his street, do you understand?'

'Yes grandad.'

'I mean it! If you see him coming near you turn around and walk the other way, avoid any contact.'

'But......!'

'No buts, I'll sort this out, not you, understand?'

'Yes grandad.'

'Right, get yourself back home, your mother will be wondering where you are and I've got work to do.'

'That'll be the day she wonders where I am.'

'Go home anyway.'

Pete gives Terry a half smile and leaves the workshop, Terry goes back to wiping his hands absent mindedly as he ponders over what Pete had just told him. He was convinced that the Harry Pete spoke of was, in fact, the Harry he knew. The mod he had tangled with all those years ago. The mod who had been the reason he went to prison. The very same one he had seen a couple of times in the last week or so. He was also fairly sure that his grandson had not told him the whole truth of his encounter with said Harry.

No matter, he knew what he was going to do.

33.

'God I remember this one.' Rita laughs she and Harry are listening to a CD called 'Mod Classics, The Early Years' the particular track playing was 'Daddy Rolling Stone' by Otis Blackwell. 'Didn't The Who do this as well?'

'They did, one of their B sides, 'Anyway, Anyhow' I think.' Harry answered.

'That was another classic, the old ones are the best. You do realise music stopped being good around 1984 don't you?'

'Oh yeah, to be honest I think it stopped being really good in 1979.'

'You reckon, that early?'

'Yeah.'

They look at each other without saying anything for a moment whilst sitting on Harry's sofa.

'Why didn't you tell Charlie about his mother the other day?'

'I don't know, I guess I'm not sure how he will take it; me poking my nose into his affairs that is.'

'I think he wants to know who and where his mother is, and would thank you for it.'

Harry reaches out and takes hold of the tips of her fingers with his. As he starts to lean closer to her the doorbell rings.

'Saved by the bell.' Rita says with a resigned tone in her voice.

'Who the hell? People do choose their moments.' Harry says as he gets up to answer the door. Don't go away.' Rita laughs.

Harry is still laughing as he opens the door but the smile is soon wiped from his face when he is confronted by Charlie with a bleeding lip.

'Can I come in?'

'Of course, Rita, it's Charlie; come on through and let's clean you up.'

'Oh my God Charlie, what happened, was it that bloody Pete again?' She stands up to take him by the shoulders and look at his split lip. 'I think it's time we called the police Harry. Come into the kitchen let me clean that wound and put some cream on it' Charlie follows Rita into the kitchen who runs a tap to wet a cloth and dab the wound.

'What happened mate?' Harry asks him.

'It doesn't matter, honestly.' Charlie replies.

'I'll have that thug Pete, this has got to stop. Rita's right, we have to call the police.'

'It won't do any good, it's not Pete and his mates.' A look of understanding spreads across Harry's face. 'He said I shouldn't come here anymore or see either of you.' With that tears start to roll down his cheek.

'You two wait here.' Harry makes his way to the front door.

'Harry, Harry, don't! Come back, Harry!' Rita calls out to him but he ignores her and storms out of the house. She looks at Charlie sympathetically.

'This isn't going to end well.' She says to an increasingly frightened Charlie.

Harry strides purposefully along the road to Charlie's house where his father is outside washing his car. He looks up to see Harry coming towards him forcefully, then drops his sponge into the bucket of soapy water to face up to the oncoming force.

'I thought you might show up.' He pushes himself forward with bravado, looking ready to take on Harry. 'Think you're a tough guy do ya? Think you're a big man? Well let me tell you I'M the big man round here, ME!' He pounds his chest with his fist as if to make his point. An elderly couple walking their dog on the other side of the road stop to watch what is going on.

'Take it easy you two, no need for any of that.' The man calls out.

'What the fuck's it got to do with you, you old fart. Piss off before I give you a slap as well.' Brian shouts at them.

'Well, really!' The Man's wife retorts, horrified, 'there's no need to be like that!'

'I told you..' Brian makes to go towards the couple but Harry steps between them. 'What'cha gonna do eh, what'cha gonna do then?'

Harry doesn't speak just stands his ground, Brian stands up to him. For a moment they just stand staring at each other. Charlie and Rita arrive on the scene having followed Harry, but don't speak.

Brian looks over to Charlie.

'Why don't you go inside boy?' He says to Charlie, 'I won't be long.' Charlie doesn't move.

Harry still doesn't speak, just bores his eyes into Brian's.

'Well say something old man.' Brian goads Harry.

Quick as a flash Harry slaps Brian's face, he staggers back with a hand to his cheek and a look of shock on his face.

'You fucker!' He shouts with surprise, 'You slapped me!'

Crack! Harry slaps his other cheek.

'I don't believe you!' Brian steps backwards with tears welling up in his eyes, Harry steps towards him and raises his hand once more but when Brian lifts his arms up to defend himself Harry drops back. 'I can't believe you fucking slapped me.'

Harry grabs Brian by the scruff of his T-Shirt and lowers his voice so that Charlie and Rita can't hear what he says.

'You think you're a big man beating your son and your wife.' Brian looks surprised, 'Oh yes I know all about what you did to Charlie's mother, he doesn't know anything, yet, but I'm about to put him in the picture. So when he comes back for his stuff you can tell him how sorry you are

'Dad?' Charlie looks towards his father then towards Rita who has her arm around him, 'Harry?'

Harry turns toward Charlie and shakes his head.

'Come with us, we've got something to tell you.'

Charlie is unresisting as Rita leads him back towards Harry's house.

'Charlie, I'm sorry son.' Brian calls out, Charlie glances back but continues to follow Rita.

'Too little too late Brian.' Harry adds as he leaves the man leaning against his car, crying.

'I really am sorry.' Brian looks towards Harry, his eyes are red with tears.'

'I know you are but it's still too late.'

Harry spins on his heel and walks away.

34.

Ed was drifting in and out of consciousness, he had been doing this for the last couple of days. At least he thought it had been a couple of days. Everything was getting more and hazier making it difficult to tell. It was only day and night he could be positive about, and even that was a bit iffy. At least it was daylight at that particular moment. The nurse had not long been around with some breakfast which he didn't really feel like eating and had left most of it. He still wasn't sure how long ago that was having drifted off a couple of times since then.

'At least when I'm dead I'll know where I am.' He whispered to himself with a quiet chuckle before he closed his eyes for a few moments, or was it more?

He came to with a start to find two people standing at the end of his bed.

'I know you,' he said whilst rubbing his eyes to focus, 'are you real or a figment of my morphine?'

'Oh I'm real enough Ed.' Terry takes off his leather jacket and puts it over the back of a chair. 'Do you mind if we take a seat?'

'And if I say I do?'

'Well I'll stand up and talk to you.'

Ed laughs.

'Oh sit down Terry you're making me feel tired. You're the last person I expected to visit me on my death bed, who's that with you?'

Terry pulls the chair closer to the bed and sits down.

'Jimmy, you probably don't remember him, he was a lot younger the last time you met.'

'In the punch up was he?'

'That's right. We heard you were in here.'

'I hope he hasn't come to pick up where we left off.' They all laugh.

'Well, I've never really had a beef with you Ed, Harry? Well that's another matter.'

'Come on Terry it's not Harry you have to blame for doing time, it's your own fault, anyway, how did you know I was here?'

'Brighton grapevine, I see people with bikes and scooters all the time in my business and they talk. I'm really sorry to see you here. Cancer's a bastard, my brother had it in the lungs and he was only fifty one. Pancreas for you, right?'

'That's' right.'

'How long?'

'I was given three to four weeks, four weeks ago so definitely on borrowed time.'

'Can't believe it was almost forty years ago since that fateful day. We weren't really looking for a fight.'

Ed raises his eyebrows.

'Really? It looked like that was exactly what you wanted, to me.'

Terry laughs.

'Yeah maybe, we wanted to rattle you mods. You know what it was like then, mods, rockers, punch up. It was history man, written in stone, mods and rockers have to fight that's what it's all about.'

'Maybe, but it got out of hand didn't it? You can't blame Harry for what happened to you.'

Terry looks down at this hands without responding.

'You didn't just come here to enquire for my health, so what did you come here for?'

'I need to ask you a favour.' Terry says without looking at Ed.

'A favour? I'm not sure I'm in any position to do you any favours, look at me. Besides, what makes you think I'd do a bloody rocker a favour let alone that rocker being you?'

Terry laughs.

'You're lucky I'm laying here or I would have cracked this table over your head.'

'I'm sure you would.' Terry laughs.

'Go on then, out with it, what do you want from me?'

'Unfinished business.'

'I'm listening.'

35.

'Are you telling me you've spoken to, seen my mum?'

'That's right Charlie, we have.' Rita replies.

'How, when?'

'I spoke to a policeman friend of mine. He found a record of the police being called to a domestic involving your mum and dad. She went to a shelter for abused women until your grandfather found a house for her.'

'But why didn't she come for me?'

'Your father said he would kill her if she ever came near you again.'

Charlie sat back in the armchair.

'I'm just trying to take it all in. My dad said he would kill my mum if she tried to contact me?'

'Yes, I don't believe he would have done, but I'm sure your mother did.' Harry answers him. 'She was also afraid for you.'

'How so?'

'Well if she was dead your father would probably be in prison and where would that leave you?'

'So why does she want me now?'

'Because she has always wanted you and there is no way your father is going to do anything bad to her now, or you, so what do you say about going to see her?'

'I, I don't know.'

'What do you have to lose by going to see her?' Rita cuts in to ask Charlie. 'I mean, you go to see her, don't like what you see and go back to your abusive father. Does that sound likely?'

'No, not really, it's just....'

'Just what?' Harry asks him.

''I don't know, it's been a long time, maybe she doesn't like what she sees.'

'Oh Charlie,' Rita laughs and reaches out to put her hand on his knee, 'she's your mother, of course she's going to like what she sees. She was so sad when we saw her, trust me she's missed you every single minute of every single day since she was forced to leave you.'

'Okay, when can we go and see her?'

'Let me make a phone call.' Harry says and gives Rita a questioning look that she understands making her nod in agreement. He picks up his mobile phone and goes into the kitchen to close the door behind him.

'Don't worry,' Rita says to Charlie, 'everything will be alright. I saw the pain in your mother's eyes when we spoke to her. The two of you are going to have a great life together.'

'Can I still see my dad?'

'Oh honey, of course you can if you want to, you're a big boy now and you can make decisions for yourself. In fact I think your parents will agree to make peace for your sake, I don't mean they will get back together but the animosity will go away and they may even be able speak to each other on a civil basis.'

'I'd like that.' Charlie replied, 'maybe dad can get rid of all that anger inside him.'

'I hope so and maybe Harry and I can help.'

'I'd really appreciate that.'

Harry came back into the room with a smile on his face.

'Right, let's get ourselves together, jump in the car and go and see your mum.'

'Really?' Beams Charlie.

'Really!' Harry answers, Charlie claps his hands and stands up to hug both Harry and Rita.

36.

As Chrissie opened the door to find Charlie on the doorstep her hands flew to her face and her body started to shake as she started to cry. They stood watching each other for a few seconds without speaking, then.

'Oh Charlie, Charlie, come here.' Charlie suddenly threw himself at his mother who wrapped her arms around him tightly. 'Oh Charlie, I've missed you so much.'

'I've missed you too mum.' Now they are both crying

'Everybody, please come in, come in.'

Harry and Rita follow to find Chrissie's father and sister waiting to rush over hug him as well.

'I don't know how to thank you two for bringing my boy back to me.' Chrissie says through the tears, 'I thought I'd never see him again.'

'We're very fond of him Chrissie,' Rita replied, 'almost as if he were our son.'

Harry gives her a look with a half-smile.

'Do you wish you'd had children Rita?'

'Very much.'

'What about you Harry?'

'Everyday Chrissie, every day.'

Chrissie notices something pass between Rita and Harry but decides not to mention it.

'Can I come and live with you mum?'

'Oh yes please, how soon can you come?'

'Well we packed a few of his things,' Harry says 'they're in the car, in a suitcase, we didn't want to presume.'

'Oh Harry you knew I would say yes.'

Harry looks embarrassed.

'Like I said, I didn't want to presume.' Chrissie smiles and puts out her hands to touch him and Rita.

'Like I said, I can't thank you enough. What about Brian, does he know where I am?'

'Don't you worry about Brian, he may have been the tough guy when he was beating on you but not when he's dealing with an old man like me. I've already had words with him but I will be explaining the situation when I go back for the rest of Charlie's gear. By the way mate you have to give me a list so I don't miss anything.'

'Do you have some paper mum so I can write something?'

'Yes, go with granddad, he'll sort something out for you.'

Charlie leaves the room with his grandfather.

'Are you sure he'll leave us alone?' Chrissie looks worried as she turns to Harry.

'Trust me Chrissie, I will sort him out for you. I'll also make my contact with the Brighton police aware of what has happened and that Charlie is now living with you.'

'You should do something about a divorce and legal custody of Charlie.' Rita adds. 'Do you have a lawyer, because if you don't I do?'

'Yes dad has one, you two will keep in touch won't you?'

'You bet.' Rita answers.

'Of course,' Harry adds, 'Charlie is very handy with engines, I suggested he finds an apprenticeship, I have an idea about that so I will definitely be in touch.'

'Here you are Harry.' Charlie comes back into the room and hands Harry a sheet of paper. 'I think I've put it all there, haven't got much anyway.'

'Leave it with me mate, we'll be back in a few days.'

'Thanks for everything Harry.'

Harry ruffles Charlie's hair and smiles.

37.

Terry is hoping to have an early day despite the fact that he has another bike to service when he finishes the one he's currently working on. Today Andy, the part timer, has the day off causing Terry to regret giving it to him. He could have been doing the other bike. So whilst heaving a heavy sigh of resignation he continues to drain the oil from the engine.

The CD player is pumping out Jerry Lee Lewis at a volume level one notch below deafening which is why Terry doesn't hear the door to the workshop open. Nor does he hear someone step inside until he goes over to turn the music off. Startled Terry spins round on his arse, grabbing a huge adjustable spanner at the same time, to see someone standing by the CD player on the other side of the room.

'You!' Terry exclaims as he brings the spanner forward in a threatening way as he slowly gets to his feet.

'Me!' Harry replies.

38.

'He's got a knife!' Ed shouts, 'leg it!'

Harry didn't need to be told twice, Ed and the others were already on their toes. Terry takes a swipe at Harry with his knife who deftly arches his body to avoid it, making his attacker lunge forward for another attempt. Harry is quicker once more, causing Terry to lose his balance and crash to the floor, allowing Harry to take off after his mates.

The other rockers, who had been momentarily dazed by the sudden burst of violence between Terry and Harry, make off after the Mods. Terry scrambles to his feet and runs to catch up with the rest of them.

Ed is at the head of the fleeing mods weaving through the lanes whilst trying desperately to avoid tourists and putting distance between him and the blood thirsty Rockers. He looks back for a second to see where his mates, and more importantly the Rockers, are. The gap seems to be closing with Harry bringing up the rear. Ed's lungs are bursting causing him to wish he'd never started to smoke.

'We're so dead,' Ed mutters to himself, 'so dead!'

He rounds a corner to be confronted by a large group of small schoolchildren and teachers milling about outside a café with tables and chairs. All this is blocking his way. He grabs his head with both hands in despair. Steve and the others arrive seconds later, the children start to cry as they are scared by the noise made by the two gangs crashing into the café furniture.

123

'What on earth is going on here?' One of the teachers demands. 'You're frightening the children.'

'Keep out of this teach'!' Terry shouts menacingly in the teacher's direction whilst brandishing his knife all around. 'It's none of your fucking business!'

'It's my business when you're frightening my children.' The teacher replies as he steps forward to confront Terry, 'Now take your fight somewhere else.'

'I said,' quick as a flash Terry punches the teacher full in the face sending him flying over the tables and chairs. He lands in a heap smack in the middle of the children, knocking some of them to the floor. 'It's none of your fucking business!'

The children start to scream and a crowd is beginning to gather around them from the shops.

'You're a fucking lunatic!' Harry shouts at Terry.

'I'm going to fucking kill you!' Terry retorts.

Up until that moment both gangs had been facing each other gasping for breath after the run. Suddenly the Rockers launched themselves at the Mods, fists flying and bike chains swinging. One of the bike chains wraps around Steve's wrist, he yanks the owner forwards and punches him in the face. The rocker lets go of the chain as he crashes to the ground, Steve now has possession of the chain which he uses on his attacker, who soon loses consciousness.

The rest of the Mods are woefully outnumbered. Steve had got lucky, but not for long as another rocker comes at him. He swings the chain at his legs, it takes him down but the chain is ripped from his hand. Bernie takes a blow to the head from a chair that he didn't see coming; what he did see was stars. Frank goes to his rescue only to have his legs kicked from under him sending him crashing into an open shop doorway to land at the feet of a salesgirl.

Ed sees an opening and goes to make a getaway but is prevented by a Rocker jumping on his back forcing him to the ground. He grabs Ed's hair and pulls his head back with the intention of smashing it into the ground. Ed rolls instead in an attempt to throw off his attacker. This isn't totally successful, but it does prevent his head contacting the ground. Steve suddenly appears to punch Ed's attacker and drag his friend away.

Meanwhile Harry and Terry are circling each other, Harry has picked up a chair in an effort to keep Terry away and prevent him from using the knife.

'I'll get you, you Mod cunt.'

'Oh yeah? Drop that knife and see who gets who.' Harry replies. As soon as he has said that a chair crashes onto his back having been thrown by one of Terry's friends. Harry is momentarily dazed and relaxes the grip on his chair, dropping his guard. Terry seizes the moment and lashes at Harry aiming to plunge the knife in his chest. Unfortunately or fortunately, depending on your point of view, as Harry falls to the ground the knife slashes across his face from his left eye to his ear.

'You fucking bastard, you've cut me, you fucking, fucking bastard.'

'Now you're going to die.'

Terry goes to lunge in for the kill.

Suddenly from nowhere a teenage girl appears and puts her arms around Harry to protect him.

'Back off you arsehole, haven't you done enough damage?'

'I'm going to kill him!'

'Don't be stupid, no you're not, in front of all these people? Do you really want to go down for murder?'

Terry hesitates.

Suddenly a bunch of policemen arrive on the scene and grab Terry and the rest of the protagonists, Harry looks up at his saviour who has pressed her handkerchief to his wound.

'Don't I know you?' He asks her.

'Didn't I tell you grabbing peoples arses would get you in trouble? So did you grab that idiot's arse as well?'

'You're her, the one from earlier.' Harry tries to laugh but winces in pain instead.

'Yeah that's me.'

'What's your name lad?' A policeman asks as he leans down to inspect Harry.

'Call and ambulance you idiot, can't you see he's bleeding badly?' The girl shouts at him.

'Don't panic love, there's one on the way. Do you know this individual?'

'We met earlier.' She replies and looks towards Harry, 'so, what's your name?'

'Harry,' he replies

'I'm Rita,' says the girl, 'pleased to meet ya.'

39.

'Harry fucking York, what the fuck do you want? I presume you've been speaking to Ed?'

'No, why? Should I?' Harry tilts his head questioningly.

'Yes, you should.'

'Why?' Harry asks looking puzzled, 'have you been to see him?'

'Yes I have, popped into the hospice the other day.'

'Why did you go to see him, didn't realise you two were bosom buddies?'

'We're not.'

'So?'

'Just go and speak to Ed. If you haven't then what are you doing here now?'

'I want a truce for the moment.'

'A truce? We've hardly been at war since the day but I hear you've been terrorising my grandson.'

'Your grandson, who's your grand..... oh is it Pete, the thug that lives near me? That would make sense.'

'Who you calling a thug?' Terry raises the spanner with menace.

'Wind your neck in Terry, it didn't work out so well for you last time did it?' Terry backs off slightly. 'I'm calling your grandson a thug, although I didn't know he was related to you, but why am I not surprised he is?'

'He's my daughter's boy, I don't see a lot of him but he swung by here and told me all about you half strangling him.'

'Well that bit's true. Look, I don't know what else he told you but I bet it's not the truth. I had to stop him and a bunch of his mates beating the crap out of another kid. He threatened me with a knife, (a trait that seems to run in the family,) which I relieved him of. Then he accosted me whilst I was with Rita outside the Concord a few nights ago. That might have gone badly had the police not been nearby.

Finally, finally he racks up on my doorstep throwing beer bottles at me. So far I have resisted beating the shit out of him but if he comes near me again I might not be able to.'

Terry lowers the spanner then goes over to place it on his workbench.

'So, yes, that's who I'm calling a thug.'

'Yeah, I guess I knew what he said about you wasn't true, not really your thing beating on kids, at least it never used to be.'

Harry slowly moves around the workshop casting his eyes around for a possible weapon, should he need one, Terry notices this.

'Relax Harry I'm not starting a fight today.'

'Someone needs to reign him in before it gets too out of hand and he does something really bad. You don't want him to end up like you did, do you?'

'No, I don't. That momentary lapse of reason cost me two years of my life.' Terry gives Harry a sad look as he shakes his head in remembrance.

'You still resent it don't you? You still blame me?' Harry barks accusingly but Terry doesn't respond. 'I ended up with face looking like a double for Boris Karloff, plus a conviction for criminal damage.'

'You didn't do time for it though, I did and not in the friendliest of nicks either. I spent the whole time in fear of my life with geezers a lot harder than me!'

'I didn't start it!' Harry retorts.

'Yes you did!' Terry spits back. 'We were just having a quiet pint when you toe rags racked up.'

'We were happy to just walk on by but you had to get in our way.' Harry is starting get angry.'

'I was just having a bit of fun with you.'

'You say that now!' Harry interrupts him.

'Then you had to go and head but me.' Terry's face is starting to go red with anger.

'Yeah, I did didn't I?' Harry starts to smile which seems to anger Terry a bit more.

'It wasn't funny, you broke my nose.'

'No Terry, you're right, it wasn't funny.'

Both men take deep breaths and calm themselves down

'Anyway, it's ancient history,' Harry adds.

'Is it? You should speak to Ed, if he's still got time.' Terry says raising his eyebrows.

Harry tilts his head to one side again.

'So why did you go and see Ed? He hasn't got much time left you know.'

'Yes, I know, you really should go and see him. Now what do you want a truce for?'

'I need a favour.' Harry curls his top lip, looks down at the floor and shuffles his feet. Terry chuckles.

'*You?* Need a favour from *me?*' Terry's eyes widen in amazement. 'Why should I do a favour for you?' His chuckling starts to get a bit louder.

'You're right, there's no reason why you'd do me a favour so let me put it another way. A friend of mine needs a favour, in fact it's the young lad your grandson was beating the shit out of the other day.'

'And what is it you think I can do for him?'

'Give him an apprenticeship.'

'What?'

'Look, he really knows his way around an engine, he helped me strip and rebuild my scooter.'

'You mean your hairdryer!' Terry quips.

'Don't start,' Harry tilts his head with a half-smile. 'He's been having a tough time, his mother disappeared over a year ago but he's just been reunited with her. He's a good lad, he needs and wants something like this. Also something tells me your Pete isn't interested in this kind of work.'

'You're right, Pete has never shown any sign of wanting to join the family business.'

Terry sighs and sits on the bike he'd been working on, Harry looked around for somewhere to park himself and finally settled on heaving himself up on the workbench after clearing it of the junk scattered over it.

'So, ignore our past and what you might think of me and consider helping this lad. Don't dismiss it just because it's me that's all I'm asking.'

'That's not the problem, 'Terry replies, 'I'm not getting any younger, a couple of years older than you I believe, and I have been looking to sell up.'

'Have you actually put it up for sale yet?' Harry asks.

'Not exactly.' Terry replies

'What does that mean?'

'I mentioned it to Dave at Brierley Autos the other day when I was there for an MOT, he said he might know someone.'

'But there's nothing serious yet?'

'No.'

'Well in that case you could maybe take him on a couple of days a week to start with. Then if someone wants to take it over you can offer him as part of the deal.'

Terry rubs his face with both hands. This is a strange situation for him. On one hand there is this deep set animosity between him and Harry, on the other hand he feels that perhaps he could do some good with this lad he's never met.

Terry breaks the silence.

'I won't promise anything, but you can send him to see me, give him the phone number here so we can sort out a time and date.'

'I can bring him.' Harry suggests.

'No, don't do that, just send him.'

Harry nods, understanding. Terry goes over to his desk to find a business card which he hands to Harry who turns it over thoughtfully in his hand.

'You're not just fobbing me off are you?' He asks quizzically whilst looking Terry in the eye.

'I wouldn't just fob you off Harry, I'd tell you to fuck off. No I mean it, most sincerely, send, what's his name?'

'Conrad, Charlie Conrad.'

'Okay, I look forward to hearing from Charlie Conrad, now fuck off and go and talk to Ed.'

Harry gives Terry a sideway look, nods his head and leaves without another word.

40.

Steve Hopkins was born in Lewisham Hospital and grew up in Catford, South London. His father, Robert, worked for the post office as counter staff and had stood as the Liberal candidate for Lewisham in the 1974 general election, although he didn't win, nor did he lose his deposit. His mother, Iris, worked in the Catford

Woolworths store and had done so since she was at school, starting as a Saturday girl, to eventually become branch manager.

He first met Harry when, at the age of five they both went to Rushey Green Primary school. They were placed next to each other on their first day and became firm friends from that day on. They had the same tastes in just about everything, especially music, so it was unsurprising when they both learnt to play the guitar and formed a band. Sadly they weren't talented enough to hit the big time but it didn't detract from their friendship. Their musical tastes led them to the mod scene and the fashions as well as the music, and the friendship of Frank, Bernie and Ed.

Over the years they had drifted apart, with Steve remaining in the area of South London. He followed his father to work for what is now The Royal Mail in the sorting office at Kings Cross. Frank and Bernie had also stayed in the South London area, with Harry and Ed transplanting to Brighton. In recent years the five of them would meet up for a reunion, at least once a year, where vast amounts of alcohol would be consumed.

He'd missed Ed at their recent reunion but had come to visit at his bedside just a few days before. Now he was once again sitting there, this time alone. Ed had deteriorated in the short time since he'd first visited, laying sleeping, and looking as if he'd lost even more weight.

One of the nurses had brought Harry and Steve cups of tea and explained that Ed slept most of the time, due to the medication. Steve suspected the morphine had a double whammy, pain relief that would gradually end his life. He didn't mind that really, it was obvious Ed was incurable. Patients aren't put into a hospice if there is a chance of a cure. So he didn't see the point in prolonging his agony by a few days. He was realistic like that, hoping that when it came to him the same compassion would be extended his way.

Ed had sent him a message, via his daughter Denise, to come and visit as he had something to tell him. Why not Harry, who lived nearby? Denise didn't know, she was just relaying her father's message. So Steve had ridden down on his scooter that morning having taken a sickie from work. Thankful he had brought that days newspaper with him and he continued to read it whilst sipping the hot tea. The nurse said it might not be best to wake Ed just yet, as he had not long gone to sleep.

That was over and hour ago and there wasn't much news left to read.

Growing impatient Steve stood up to lean over the sleeping Ed to whisper quietly.

'Ed, Ed, it's me Steve, I'm here mate, you wanted to see me, come on wakey, wakey.'

Ed stirs a little bit but keeps sleeping, Steve is beginning to get frustrated. On one hand he was thinking he had better things to do than to sit listening to Ed snoring, then, chastising himself for thinking that way when his friend is dying. This time he places his hand on Ed's arm to gently shake it.

'Ed, Ed come mate I'm dyi....er eager to hear what you want to tell me.'

This time Ed begins to stir.

'That's it mate, wake up.' Ed's eyelids flutter as he slowly comes to. 'Hello, hello, here I am, rushing to your bedside, waiting with baited breath to hear your pearls of wisdom.'

'Steve,' he is unable to sit up, 'thanks for coming, have you been here long?' Ed still attempts to sit up but Steve puts his hand to his chest to dissuade him from trying anymore.

'No, not long, just started reading the paper.'

'Anything earth shattering in there?'

'Nah, same old shit, Prime Minister says we've never had it so good while the other bugger says we ain't' Ed attempts a laugh. 'Does it hurt much?' Steve asks him.

'Only when I laugh.' They both chuckle at that. 'You managed to get the day off all right then?'

'Chucked a sickie didn't I? Anyway I'm the boss who's going to question me? Been there so long now I'm part of the furniture.' Ed attempts to laugh again but it's obvious the pain is getting to him, he tries to reach down to click a dose of his medication but the effort is too much for him.

'Here, let me do it.' Steve reaches over.

'Give me a double dose mate.'

'Is that all right?'

'What are they going to do if it isn't?' Steve smiles.

'Shall I make it three then?'

'Why not.' Steve clicks the injector three times which makes Ed feel better almost immediately.

'Thanks mate, I'll miss this stuff, its best I've ever had.' They both chuckle at the thought.

'So, what have you brought me all the way down here for, not just to top up your morphine I guess?'

'I had a visit from Terry.' Steve sits back down with his eyes widening in surprise.

'You mean Terry the knife man?'

'The very same.'

'Wow, now I wasn't expecting that! What did he want, to make sure you were on the way out?' Ed frowns, 'Sorry mate that was really insensitive of me, so what did he want?'

'Don't tell Harry but Terry and I have sort of kept in touch over the years. I never told any of you but I went to visit him in Portland nick not long after he was sent down.'

'What? You even gave evidence against him at the trial, why would you do that?'

'I felt sorry for him.'

'YOU FELT SORRY,' Steve realised he was almost shouting, 'sorry, sorry, you felt sorry for him? He missed Harry's eye by a cat's whisker and left him looking like a survivor from a medieval duel. What exactly did you feel sorry for?'

'He was just a kid like we were, it all got out of hand, especially when Harry head butted Terry.'

'That didn't give him the right to cut Harry, he could have killed him!'

'Harry started it!'

'Calm down Ed, I didn't come here to argue over ancient history. What did Terry want?'

'He wants to pick up where we left off.'

'He wants to what?'

'He wants to pick up where we left off.'

'And what does that mean exactly?'

'He wants us to have a fight, like we did all those years ago, no knives or weapons of any kind, just knuckle sandwiches.'

'Are you mad? Is he mad? We're all fucking pensioners and you certainly can't take part, what's the point?'

'Unfinished business he says.'

'And if we say fuck off, which I hasten to say is what I'm certainly saying.'

'He's thrown down the gauntlet and challenging us, do you want to lose face?'

'I think I can afford to lose this one.'

Ed tries to laugh but the pain gets to him.

'Speak to the others.'

'Really? Are you serious? They're all going to tell me to fuck off when they've finally stopped laughing.'

'I bet Harry won't.'

'Well, maybe not but I can't see Frank and Harry signing up for Zimmer frames at twenty paces.'

'Will you at least speak to them?'

'Okay,' Steve sighs, 'I'll talk to them, but that means there'll be four of us, how many of them are there?'

'Terry said he'd match number for number.'

'Oh this is fucking insane, we're not kids, this was forty years ago.' Steve sinks back in his chair and looks over to Ed. 'You're fucking mad, he's fucking mad, we're all fucking mad! I haven't seen the fucker since the trial, not sure I'd know him if I fell over him.'

They both start to laugh.

'Funnily enough he hasn't changed much, just got a bit older like the rest of us. Still riding a bike.'

'I came down on my scooter today, just felt like giving it an airing.'

'Glad to hear it's still running, I took mine to bits years ago, just gave it all to Harry.'

'Yeah we all saw him a couple of days ago down at the front with the young lad who helped him rebuild it.'

The two men fell silent for a few moments/

'I suppose you want me to tell Harry.'

41.

'So that's what Terry meant when he said speak to Ed?' Harry said to Steve as he handed him a can of beer from the fridge.

'What do you mean, have you spoken to Terry?'

'Yeah. I stopped by his workshop the other day, needed to ask him to do something for me.'

'And what would he do for you, after you sent him to jail for two years?'

'That's my business.'

'Did he say he would?'

'That's my business too.'

'But he never mentioned calling us out?'

'No he didn't, he did say that he'd been to see Ed, and that they'd been keeping in touch over the years. Ed even went to visit the bastard in jail, can you believe that?'

'He did what?' Said Steve, pretending he didn't know.

'Yeah, visited him in jail. The arsehole, bastard, fucking, cunt who gave me this.' Harry point to his scar.

'So, that's the same arsehole, bastard, fucking, cunt you just asked for a favour?'

'The very same.' They both laugh.

Steve had come directly from visiting Ed in the hospice, in the hope that he would find Harry at home.

'Have you spoken to Frank or Bernie yet?'

'No I came straight to you, being as how you're close by that is, and having more than enough reason to actually want to do this crazy thing.'

'Do you?'

'I don't know, not really, do you?'

'The nineteen year old in me is chomping at the bit, however the pensioner is saying don't be fucking stupid.' Harry moves over to the sofa and motions Steve to take a seat.

'I know it's mad, it's all right for Ed to say do it, he's not in any fit shape to take part, which leaves four of us. And if the other two say no way that just leaves you and me.' Steve observes.

'I haven't said I'm in yet, that leaves you.' Harry replies.

'Mate I think it's you he really wants, he won't give a damn if the rest of us are there or not.'

Harry drums his finger on his knee while contemplating the situation.

'If he wanted to do me that much he could have caved my head in with the spanner he had in his hand when I was at his workshop, but he didn't.'

'I don't think the idea is to kill you, just, well maybe close to it, just retribution for the jail time.'

'Do you think he's owed it?'

'No of course not, just saying that's what he is probably thinking.'

Harry continues to drum his fingers on his knee.

'Best you phone the others and arrange a meet.' Harry says to Steve whilst still drumming his fingers, Steve picks up Harry's phone to make that call. After making them he hangs up and turns back to Harry.

'They can both make it down here tomorrow evening.'

'Well you'd better bunk down on the sofa tonight, not a lot of sense going back home now to come back tomorrow.'

'Okay, let's get drunk, I'll pop out for a bottle of something you call out for a couple of pizzas, El Diablo for me.'

'With extra chilli?' Steve smiles.

'Absolutely.' Harry smiles back.

Harry lets Steve out and pours himself another whisky which he sinks in one go then pours another. His mind is in turmoil, wondering if he backs out of the fight Terry is asking for, he won't help Charlie. Should he even put himself on the line in this way, just to help some kid he barely knows?

'Call Rita.' He mutters, picks up the phone and starts to dial but stops before punching in the last number and hangs up. 'Maybe not, well not yet anyway'

He sips on the whisky still turning the situation over in his head whilst pacing back and forth. He turns on the TV and sits down for a couple of seconds before standing up again to pace the room some more and finish the whisky, pouring yet another one - not taking in what was on the TV.

'Get drunk he said, ha, at this rate I'll be drunk before he gets back. Shit! Pizza!'

Having suddenly remembered to order the pizza, Harry digs out the take away menu and dials their number to make the order.

In no time Steve arrives back with the whisky and some cans of Guinness, while a little bit later the pizza lands. Harry pours them a glass of the black stuff each and opens the pizza boxes on the table. They're both hungry and attack the pizzas ravenously without speaking for a few minutes.

'Remember that day? You know, that day.' Steve says with a half full mouth of El Diablo. 'Do you regret it?'

'Every single day.'

'If you could do it again?'

'I wouldn't.'

'What would you do differently?'

'I'd turn around and walk the other way.'

'And what do you think they would have done?'

'Well it was all down to Terry, he was the leader of the gang. I think he would have called us a bunch of wimps and the rest of them would have laughed and jeered at us. So, we, no my young self wouldn't have taken that and we'd have fought anyway. If my sixty year old self could have been there it would have been different.'

'Yeah well, it's all ancient history now.'

'Obviously not for Terry.'

'Maybe I should go and speak to him, say how stupid all this is.'

'No mate, at the very least I should face him down, if it starts to go bad for me maybe you can break it up.'

'So you're going to do it?'

'Ask me again when I've sobered up.' With that Harry refills their whisky glasses and picks up another piece of pizza. 'If I sober up that is.' He laughs, swallows the single malt and then takes a bite of the pizza.

Steve raises his glass in a toast and laughs.

'Not sure if I will either.' Steve says then swallows the drink in one go. Harry refills both their glasses.

'A lot of water has flowed under the bridge since that fateful day mate.' Harry says nodding his head at the same time.

'And a lot of whisky.' Steve adds, 'and a lot of Guinness.' They laugh even more. 'I was really sad when you moved down here. You're my best mate, that's never changed even though I don't see you that often. That's why I'm here now, I don't want you to do this but I understand why you do and I'll support you all the way.'

'Thanks Steve, you know I love you mate, we've known each other for over fifty years now. Whatever happens with this madness we need to get together more often, we don't know how much time we've got'

Steve frowns.

'What are you saying?'

'Nothing, just, we're not getting any younger either of us and we should make the best of whatever time we have left.'

'Is there something you're not telling me?'

Harry hesitates for a brief second.

'No, of course not, it's just what with Ed having so few days left we should make the effort.'

'What about that tooth of yours, had it out yet?'

'No, the tooth fairy gave me some anti-biotics, not supposed to drink with them but the swelling is still going down, slowly. I'll think about having it out if the pain comes back.'

'It will mate, bite the bullet and have it out, you know it makes sense.'

'Maybe,' it was obvious to Steve that Harry didn't want to talk about it.

'How about putting some Jam on the CD player, we're not actually watching TV are we?' Steve asks, changing the subject. 'If we're going to get drunk we need to listen to some great sounds, you've got all their stuff I presume?'

'Of course. Gimme a minute.' He turns off the TV and sorts through his CD's. 'So, let's start at the beginning shall we, In the City?'

'Yeah fab!' Harry puts the disc in the player and hits the play button, as the opening bars of 'Art School' fill the room they are both transported back to the days when they first heard this album. 'Jeez this brings back memories.' Steve reminisces.

'Those were the days,' Harry adds as he turns the volume up another notch.

'Remember the gig at the Hammy Odeon?'

''Burnt into my memory, I've still got the poster on the garage wall.'

'The poster! I couldn't believe you got them to sign it, even that miserable bastard Weller.'

'Eventually! When the other two twisted his arm.'

They both laugh at the memory.

'Make sure you leave it to me in your will.' Steve laughs and Harry smiles

''You can rely on it.' Harry replies continuing to smile. Steve notices something in the way he looks but doesn't pick up on it, just continues to laugh.

'Where did all the years go mate?' Steve asks him.

'They just slipped away without us noticing.' Harry replied, 'it seems like last week we first sat down next to each other in Rushey Green. I can still see that day as clear as if it were yesterday, all those kids crying for their mothers while you and I didn't stop talking.'

'Right, I so felt sorry for Miss, shit what was her name?'

'Giles, Miss Giles.'

'Of course, Miss Giles, having to deal with the two of us talking non-stop while trying to calm down the sobbing babies.'

'Do you remember some of the other kids?' Harry asks him.

'Yeah, who was that kid who sat behind us in the second year who kept drinking ink out of the ink well? His mouth was constantly blue and he would keep saying the word 'motion' because his mother used it to ask if he'd had a crap.'

'Oh no, right, he was Mark something.'

'You're right, Mark something, and his mate Morris something.'

'Yeah, now I've got it, Mark Stanley, what a weird geezer he was, don't remember Morris' other name either.'

'Surprised I can remember that much.'

'And the other teachers, big Miss Jones.'

'And little Miss Jones!' Harry remembers as the two of them continue to laugh.

'What about that teacher who locked you in the classroom after school had finished?'

'Oh right, how could I forget Miss Stevens! I spilt red paint all down my leg and she made me stand in the corner behind the door. Then forgot about me and I was too scared to go, even after the class had emptied. It wasn't until the cleaners came and I was still standing in the corner that I was let out. Mum was furious and gave Stevens a real tongue lashing.'

'Those were the days. Here.' Steve held his glass out for some more whisky, Harry emptied his and refilled both of them.

Steve stood up and went over to the photographs on the wall, and picked up the one of the five of them back in the day.

'This was taken the next time we came to Brighton, your scar is really noticeable then.'

Harry was just about to make a comment when the telephone rang. He held up is hand to stop Steve from speaking as he answered it.

'Hello, oh hi Denise, everything all right?' He listened for a few minutes and leant against the wall. 'Thanks for letting me know, Steve's here at the moment, I, I'll call you back.'

He hung up.

'Ed's gone.'

42.

138

The atmosphere in the pub is sombre, Harry and Steve have just arrived, Harry is buying a round of drinks for everyone and hands them out.

'To Ed!' Harry lifts his glass.

'To Ed!' they echo together.

'He wouldn't have wanted us to be sad.' Bernie says quietly.

'No, he wouldn't.' Frank adds solemnly.

'Maybe, but I am anyway.' Says Steve.

'He was the quiet one of us.' Said Harry.

'Yeah and I would tease him about it constantly.' Steve added.

They all go quiet.

'Come on, this isn't the wake yet.' Frank attempts to liven up the atmosphere. 'We came here to talk about what he wants us to do.'

'Was he serious?' Bernie asks.

'I spoke to Ed myself, the day he died and he was very serious. I went from his bedside to Harry's place, which is where I phoned you two from, as you know. Terry had come to see him only days before and Ed emphasised he had been serious.'

'It's fucking stupid, we're not kids anymore.' Bernie replied.

'Why did he go to Ed?' Franks asked.

'Because they had kept in touch with each other.' Steve replied.

'Ed even visited him in the nick!' Harry added, 'he never told us that, did he?' Harry shook his head, looking away from the others and into his beer. 'And after what he did.'

'It makes sense,' Steve injects 'I mean there's a lot of bad blood between us; he knew he could get a message to us through Ed.'

'But he's old like we are.' Frank says with a note of indignation in his voice.'

'Frank's got a good point.' Bernie pipes up, 'I have to piss every ten minutes these day, my backs shot and my knees are in constant pain. I bet you you've all got some kind of pains, for fuck sake we are not kids, this is fucking stupid.'

'Maybe we can try and get a few more of the old Mods out for the day.' Steve suggests.

'Like who? Everyone has jobs, families, kids, grandkids, a hundred reasons to laugh this off.' Frank says.

'I don't know off the top of my head but....' Steve replies.

'But nothing, this is daft beyond recognition.' Said Bernie.

'This is Ed's fault, he should have told Terry to fuck off when he asked him to do this.' Frank adds.

'No, it's not Ed's fault, it's mine.' Harry leans forward in his seat. 'I started this all those years ago, a cocky little shit who wanted to show a bunch of rockers who the boss was. I head butted him without thinking about the consequences and I have to deal with them now.'

'For Christ's sake Harry you're more likely to give yourself a bloody heart attack before you do any damage to Terry.'

'Maybe, we just never finished what we, sorry, I mean I started, so now is the time.'

'I don't believe I'm hearing this.' Bernie says angrily.

'This feud between them goes way back.' Steve says.

'Fine, let them beat the shit out of each other, why the fuck should we get dragged into it?' Bernie is getting even angrier.

'Because we're his mates.' Steve replies.

'Yes we are,' Frank softens.

'What?' Bernie looks around at them all. 'This is fucking ridiculous.'

'We're a gang.' Frank adds.

'Yeah, we meet up now and then, drink a few beers, well too many beers, listen to some Jam and Small Faces on the juke box, reminisce and go home till the next time. It's the past Frank, when we were young and stupid, not the present when we are supposed to be old and wise.'

'He offered us out Bernie.' Steve adds calmly.

'We'd get arrested.' Bernie observes,

'I don't mean we should go back to the scene of the crime to re-enact it, we'll go up on the downs, far away from the old bill.' Harry suggests.

'This is fucking bonkers,' states Bernie.

'Yes, it is Bernie, you're right of course.' Harry agrees as he sits back down again. 'That's what we are, bonkers, maybe our lives are almost over, perhaps they are, but can't we go down fighting?'

They all go quiet for a few moments, each taking a sip of their beer.

'All the more reason to ride out one last time,' says Steve, 'the Mods last stand.' He laughs at the thought.

'What do you say?' Harry asks.

'I'm in.' Frank says.

'This is stupid and childish, count me out!' Bernie finishes his beer, gets up and makes to leave. Harry stands up a grabs his arm.

'You'll come to Ed's funeral though won't you?'

'Of course I will, just give me a call when you know when it will be.' Bernie looks angry.

'Sure,' Harry nods and let's go of Bernie's arm allowing him to put on his coat and leave the pub without looking back.

'So, it's the magnificent three then.' Steve quips.

'Looks like it.' Harry replies as the pub door closes.

43.

It's just after ten in the morning, the day after the meeting with the gang. Harry is making himself some tea when the doorbell rings. As he wasn't expecting anyone he picks up his baseball bat and gingerly opens the door to two policemen.

'Good morning Harry.' The policeman at the front speaks to him, 'expecting trouble are you?' The officer frowns as he looks at the bat in Harry's hand.

'You could say that,' Harry replies, 'but hopefully not from you two.'

'No, not today, we just need your help with something, can we come in?'

Harry steps aside to let them both in.

'Of course you can Jim, who's your friend?'

'This is Constable Williams, Nick to his friends, he's a new boy I'm breaking in.'

'Pleased to meet you Nick, how long have you been in the job?'

'Couple of months now.' Harry closes the front door and ushers the two coppers into his lounge.

'Enjoying it?' Harry asks him.

'So far.' Nick replies.

'Can I get you anything, tea or coffee?' Harry offers.

'No thanks Harry.'

'What can I do for you then Jim?'

Jim opens the folder he's carrying with him.

'Do you remember this lad?' He pulls out a photograph and passes it over to Harry who recognises him immediately.

'How could I forget, if you hadn't happened along at the time things could have turned out nasty for me.'

'Oh I don't think it would have turned out nasty for you, maybe for him, but not you.' Jim gives a small chuckle at the thought of Harry getting the better of the situation.

'Maybe, but why do you ask?'

'Do you know who he is?'

'Why, what has he done?'

'Do you know him?'

'I've come across him more than once, none have been particularly pleasant.'

'What are your experiences of him?'

'Well, the first time was when I stopped him beating the crap out of another young lad, the second time when you were there and last time he was throwing bottles at me.'

'Who is he?'

'I only know his first name, Pete.'

'Where does he live?'

'Can't help there, but I don't think it's too far from here as it was in the alleyway up the road where I found him beating the other kid.'

'Who was the other kid?'

I don't know, he ran off when I stopped what was happening. So tell me what has he done?'

'After he left you the other night he mugged an old couple for the princely sum of fifteen quid. The woman had a heart attack.'

'Jesus!' Harry sat down, shocked. 'Is she all right?'

'Touch and go at the moment, she's in intensive care, it's not looking good.'

'That's terrible, for fifteen nicker, you're sure it was him?'

'No doubt, the husband picked him out of the mugshots. I had a feeling it may have been him so I added his picture.'

Harry ran his fingers through his hair thoughtfully.

'Are you all right sir?' Nick asked him, 'you're looking a bit white in the face.'

'Er yes Nick, no worries, just a bit shocked that this could happen in Brighton.'

'Happens quite a lot Harry,' Jim adds. 'Are you sure you don't know where we can find him?'

'As I said, I saw him not far from here so I would expect if you look hard enough, you'll come across him.'

'Well, if you should see him again, please give the station a call. If she dies it could be murder, or manslaughter at the very least.'

'Yes, yes, of course I will.'

'Need to get these thugs off the streets sir, Can't have decent people robbed while having a leisurely stroll up the pier can we?'

No Nick, we can't'

With that he shows the two policeman out.

'Little shit!' Harry mutters to himself and goes to the telephone book where he looks up the number for Terry's garage, then dials it. He almost hangs up as the phone rings for quite some time but eventually Terry's voice answers it.

'Weisman's Autos.'

'Terry, its Harry York.'

'Harry, I take it you've spoken to Ed?'

'No, Ed died two days ago.'

'I'm sorry to hear that, he was a decent fella.'

'Yes he was.'

'When is the funeral?'

'Next Tuesday, two o'clock.'

'Okay thanks for letting me know.'

'That's not why I called.'

'The fight?'

'No, we'll talk after the funeral, no it's about your grandson.'

'What about him? Has he given you more trouble? Surely you can handle him?'

'No, he may have killed someone.'

Terry goes quiet on the other end of the line.

'Are you serious?'

'Sorry, yes I'm afraid I am. I've just had the police on my doorstep. They saw him with me at the Who's Who gig at the weekend. Seemingly after he left me he mugged an old couple and the woman had a heart attack. She's still alive but it's not looking good.'

'How do they know it's him?'

143

'They took his photograph when he was with me and showed it to the husband who identified him.'

'What did you tell the police?'

'I just said I knew his name was Ed but I didn't know where he lived. They're going to catch up with him eventually Terry, I just wanted to give you the heads up. It might be better if you take him in to give himself up. I know he didn't mean to hurt the woman, it'll go better for him if he does, even if she doesn't make it through, he can't run forever.'

Terry goes quiet, Harry hangs on the other end, waiting for a reaction.

'Thanks for letting me know Harry, I appreciate you not giving him up, I'll sort this out. I'll see you at the funeral.'

With that the line went dead leaving Harry standing with the receiver in his hand.

44.

Nobody enjoys going to a funeral and this particular one was no exception. February may well be close to rolling over into March but the weather wasn't improving in a big way. Why does it always rain at a funeral? Well, okay, it just seems to always rain. On the day of Ed's funeral however, it was snowing. Not really unusual for this time of the year but perhaps it would have been more acceptable if it hadn't. Snow was preferable to rain, there's something a little bit cleaner about snow, less depressing. It had in fact been snowing all the night before and was now a few centimetres deep on the floor of the cemetery.

The thick blanket of the white stuff however hadn't deterred the large number of Ed's friends from attending his funeral. Harry, Steve, Frank and the reluctant Bernie were there of course plus a contingent of South London Mods who had arrived on scooters, snow or no snow, clan in Zoot Suits. Ed had been the manager of a large hotel in Brighton, having worked his way up from being a bell boy almost forty years before. He would still have been there were it not for the cancer that overtook him so swiftly. The hotel had left a skeleton staff to allow as many as possible to attend his last stand.

There were also a large number of regular guests, some of them famous faces, who had made the effort to attend as well. Denise felt sad and proud at the same time that her father had been so well respected in the community. She had asked Harry to give the eulogy, a non-religious one due to Ed's atheist beliefs. Despite the fact that he felt honoured he declined at first. He said there were far better people who could a far better job but she was adamant that he should do it.

Harry arrived early at the crematorium with Rita, Charlie and the gang. People began arriving not long afterwards,

'Nice of you to come Charlie, despite never having met Ed.' Steve shakes his hand.

'I wanted to support you all, I was honoured to meet you and really sorry I never had the opportunity to meet Ed as well.' Charlie replies.

Steve looks over Charlie's shoulder to a group of bikers who pull into the car park.

'I don't fucking believe it.' He says in surprise.

'What?' Harry looked round at him.

'Look, Terry and a bunch of bikers, fucking cheek.' Steve goes to make a move towards them.

'Calm down Steve,' Harry puts his arm out to prevent Steve from going any further. 'This is Ed's funeral, everyone is welcome to pay their respects and that includes Terry and co. It is not our place to decide who can and who can't, we are NOT going to upset Denise by making a scene.'

'But he called us out.' Steve says indignantly.

'And we haven't accepted, yet.'

'Yea but…!'

'But nothing, today is a truce, you will not make a scene.'

'What are you talking about?' Charlie asks, 'you sent me to have an apprenticeship with Terry, I don't understand.'

'Neither do I.' Rita buts in, 'I think you have some explaining to do.'

'Not now Rita, I have to go and speak to him, wait here, all of you.' He looks meaningfully at them all. 'It'll be all right.'

Steve looks at him and shakes his head.

'If you say so.'

'I do.'

With that Harry goes over to Terry and the gang of bikers.

'Terry.'

'Harry.'

'Thanks for coming, Ed would have appreciated it.'

'You said you didn't speak to him?'

'No I didn't, I was too late, but Steve did and I got the message.'

'So what do you say?'

'Thanks for taking on Charlie.'

'He seems like a good lad, even if he seems to be leaning towards being a Mod.'

'Is that such a bad thing?'

'Nah, but given time I might convert him.'

'Maybe.'

'So what about the challenge?'

'Sorry, you mean the adolescent invitation to a punch up?'

'If you put it that way, yes.'

'How can we refuse?'

Terry smiles.

'Let me know where and when.'

'Count on it.'

With that Harry turns on his heels and makes his way back to Rita and the others, she is looking angry.

'Are you mad?' Rita asks while shaking her fist in Harry's direction.

'Ah right, so someone has put you in the picture.'

'Yes someone has put me in the bloody picture, are you insane? You're not a kid anymore.'

'I said, we'll talk about it later. Now come on, there's a huge crowd here now, a lot more than I was expecting.'

'Is everything all right Harry?' Denise suddenly arrives behind them, Harry is startled and turns around to face her.

'Yes sweetheart, everything is fine, nice turn out.'

'Yes, I'm overwhelmed, dad would have been proud.'

'That he would, and your mother would be especially proud of you. Come on let's go inside.'

'Are you okay with the eulogy?'

'Scared stiff if I'm honest but for Ed I'm going to be very brave.'

Denise touches his arm and smiles.

'Thanks Harry, whatever you say, or don't say will be fine with me. I know dad is up there looking down on us and having a good laugh.'

Denise's' husband comes out of the chapel of rest.

'Everybody's in now darling, Harry, we're all waiting for you.'

'We're coming, ready Harry?' She asks him.

'Right behind you sweetheart.'

Harry followed Denise into the chapel of rest, music was playing, The Jam's 'Going Underground', of course. Harry smiles at the thought of Ed insisting on this being played at this funeral. He made a mental note to let Rita know what he wanted played at his own funeral. This was a very apt track.

People were still seating themselves. Denise had produced a nice four page leaflet with some photographs of Ed and her mother plus some of Denise as a child. Harry smiled at them, remembering the day he had met him, some years after he'd met Steve. This time when they were both eleven. Having moved on to the senior school.

With his heart pounding in his chest Harry stood up to the podium to look over the large crowd who had come to pay their respects to his old friend.

'I doubt anything like this many will come to see me off.' He muttered soulfully to himself. He waits patiently as everyone settles down and the room goes quiet.

'First of all let me thank you on behalf of Ed, Denise, Sammy and myself for taking the time to come here to pay your respects. There's a lot of you I don't know and some I do, you know who you are and again I thank you for coming, no matter what.'

With that he looked pointedly at Terry and his crew, takes a breath then continues.

'I first met Ed when we were eleven years old and started school together at Forest Hill School. For those of you not from South London it's in the Lewisham area, if you don't know that, well...'

There is a murmur of amusement.

'We became firm friends from day one and together with Steve, Frank and Bernie,' Harry waves his hand in the general direction of his three friends, 'we became inseparable. Our mutual love of music from the mod scene, together with its fashions, eventually led us to all buying a scooter. Something the five of us still have, well I've got what's left of Ed's.'

Another murmur of amusement.

'It was these scooters that first brought us to Brighton, somewhere that would capture Ed's heart as would, not long after, his lovely wife Sheila. A match made in heaven that produced a lovely daughter in Denise and now the next generation in Sammy.

Ed was a gentle soul who saw the good in everybody, something I often had trouble coming to terms with. They say the good die young, if that is the case then Ed proves the point. He was a good man, you only have to look around this room to see how many people agree with me and he has certainly been taken from us far too early.

We didn't see as much of each other as we should have done in recent years but he was always there for me if I needed him. I was always there for him too, although he never called on me for any help. I like to think he never needed it, if he did I suspect there are plenty here who would have risen to the challenge.

You don't need me to tell you his life story as most of you know it. I will just say that Ed was my friend for the best part of forty years and will sorely miss him.

Thank you for time and listening to me, it was an honour to speak for Ed. He had a saying, which is as true today as it was the first time he used it. To be seen, stand up, to be heard, speak up but to be appreciated, shut up.'

The audience laughs.

Harry steps down to take his place next to Denise with the rest, as the coffin is taken through the curtains to the sounds of The Jam's 'That's Entertainment'.

'I presume Ed chose the music?' Harry asks her.

'How did you guess?' Denise smiles at him, 'Thanks for your kind words about dad.'

'No problem, I found it difficult to say anything, I'm sorry I didn't say more.'

'You did well, no worries.'

The mourners file out of the room to either make their way to the wake or look in wonder at the vast amount of flowers to be found in the garden. Harry slips away from the crowd to make his way over to a grave nearby.

The headstone is clean and undamaged, the grave itself is neat, well kept in fact with fresh flowers in the jar placed upon it.

The inscription reads.

'Robert Harold York, much loved son of Rita and Harold rest in Peace.'

Harry fights back the tears he can feel welling up in his eyes as he kneels down to reach out and touch the stone. However he is unable to do so and his body begins to heave with heavy sobbing.

'Not a happy day today son, missing you more than ever.'

'No, not a happy day today.' A voice comes from behind as a hand gently rests on his shoulder, Harry doesn't need to turn around, if he didn't know Rita's voice by now he never will. 'I knew I would find you here.' She says.

'I come here a lot.' Harry says as he chokes on his tears whilst trying to compose himself.

'I know you do, so do I.' Rita starts to cry as well. 'You think I don't know who brings the fresh flowers?'

Harry stands up and they throw their arms around each other tightly and cry together.

'My mother used to say that he was a fragile child from the day he was born.' Says Harry.

'He was that,' Rita replies.

'But he was, he was so, so bloody special.'

'Yes, he was.'

They both go quiet for a few moments, the snow begins to ease up but neither of them had really noticed that it had been heavier. They pull apart but continue to hold hands as they look into each other's eyes.

'You're seeing him in Charlie aren't you?' Harry doesn't answer immediately, 'Maybe you were thinking that this was how Robbie would have been at Charlie's age.'

Harry goes to sit on the headstone and looks up at Rita.

'Yeah maybe, sort of, oh I don't know, it just felt like, well with you being there with him, visiting his mother, sorting out that situation, it all felt so…… Do you understand?'

'Yes, I think so.'

'It just reminds me of what we lost, not just Robbie, we lost each other, I lost you.' Harry says while still trying to hold back the tears.

'You really lost yourself babe. When he was first diagnosed with leukaemia we lived in hope that he would be able to beat it.'

'Then the Chemo seemed to make it worse.'

'Yes it did and we looked so hard to find a donor but he just continued to slip away and then….'

'And then he died.' Harry said as he hung his head and started to sob some more.'

'Yes, he did and then you went away, retreated into yourself. I tried to reach out to you but you just pushed me away. I needed my husband so, so much but you just weren't there, your body was but not your soul and I needed your soul more than anything else.'

'I'm so sorry.'

'I know.'

'I put you through so much more pain then, more than you were already getting with Robbie's death.'

'I'm not angry anymore Harry.'

'I still love you Reet, you know I do, I could never stop.'

'I know you do.'

'And what about me?'

'I'm sorry Harry, I'll always love you but not like it used to be. I can't not feel something, too much has happened between us for that but.......'

'I know.'

'I wish I could, I really do but it's too late, too much water under the bridge. But I will always be here for you, we're still friends aren't we?'

'Always Reet, always and I'm always here for you as well.' With that Harry stands up again and looks back to the grave. 'He gave us nine wonderful years didn't he?'

'That he did darling that he did.' With that Rita takes his hand again.

'He was one of the good ones.' Harry says.

'Yes he was, and he never complained about his situation, always joking.'

'He would have made a great stand-up comic. Remember that joke he was always telling, said it was his favourite?'

'The one about Saddam Hussain you mean?' Rita laughs at the thought, Harry laughs too.

'Yes that's the one, Englishman. Scotsman and an Irishman had to sing a song about dogs. The Irishman sings Strangers in the Night and Saddam says it's not about dogs and Paddy says wait till you get to the chorus and sings 'Scooby doobie do'

With that they both burst into laughter and tears at the same time. Harry kisses his finger tips and touches the headstone.

'Happy birthday son.' He says.

Rita does the same.

'Happy birthday son.' Rita says as well.

'Weird Ed's funeral should be today.' Harry muses.

'It's almost as if he knew.' Rita adds.

'Crafty old bastard wasn't he?'

'More than we knew I think. Come on we've got a wake to go to.' Rita smiles, hooks her arm through Harry's and pulls him away back to the car park. 'We'll come back again, together next time, don't think of coming here without me.'

'I won't!' Harry replies and allows her to guide him back to her car.

45.

The wake was held in Ed's local pub, there were far too many people to have it in his daughter's house. Rita had volunteered to do the catering, ably assisted by Sara who had been holding the fort until everyone arrived. Rita and Harry were among the first to arrive, because she was in charge of the food and he was riding with her. Harry ordered a large whisky and sank it in one go.

'Needed that did you?' Rita asked.

'Yes I did.'

'I'd like one too but I have to drive.'

'One won't hurt, especially as it will be some time before you have to drive.'

Rita thought about that for a moment.

'You're right, two large whiskies please.' She called to the barman.

'Ice, water?' He asked.

'Straight!' Harry and Rita said together.

'To Robbie,' Harry lifted his glass.

'To Robbie,' Rita met Harry's eyes and then drank the amber liquid in one go. Rita coughed as it burnt its way down her throat, Harry smiled.

They had driven in a tense silence all the way back from the crematorium. Rita had asked once what was going on with Terry but Harry just mumbled that they would talk about it later. Rita was not amused.

'When are you going to tell me what is going on with you and Terry?' She asked as she put her empty glass back on the bar.

151

'When today is over and done with.' With that he orders another whisky and walks away to greet people coming through the door. In just a short time Terry and his crew arrive, Rita watches as they pass Harry, who gives them a perfunctory nod without shaking any hands. They make their way over to the bar, Rita watches Harry continue to stand by the door so she makes her way up to Terry who turns to greet her.

'Rita, long time no see, how are you?'

'Surprised to see you,' She replies, then nods in the direction of the others, 'and this lot here.'

'I'm sure you are, however you probably don't know that Ed and I kept in touch over the years.'

Rita raises her eyebrows.

'How so?'

'He realised everything got out of hand on that day way back when and came to visit me in jail.'

Rita's eyes widened even further.

'You're fucking joking!'

'No joke, we had a beer now and then, I respected him.'

'Harry was right, Ed was too soft for his own good.'

'Maybe.'

'So what's all this I hear about you calling him out?'

'Unfinished business.'

'That's a crock, unfinished business my arse, you still blame Harry for your spending two years in the nick.'

'No, you're wrong, that was my fault, I admit it, I just think I could have beaten him, without the knife.'

'And you want to pick up where you left off, forty years after the day?'

'That's about the size of it.'

'You're fucking mad and Harry's even more so if he's even thinking about doing this. If I have anything to do with it this won't happen.'

'Good luck with that Rita.'

'You should be grateful, if it hadn't been for me you would have been doing life instead of two years.'

'Yeah, I know.'

Rita, seething, whirls round and stomps away from Terry and throws a glaring look over at Harry who can feel her penetrating look as he glances over to her.

'Shit!' Harry says to himself as he realises she now knows what is going on between him and Terry. 'Time to bite the bullet.' He adds and makes his way over to her.

'If I didn't know you better I'd think you were serious about doing this.' Rita hisses as she grabs hold of the collar on Harry's jacket, dragging him out of earshot of the others.

'What can I say?'

'Say you're not going to do this.'

'I wish I could.'

'Why can't you?'

'It's not just about me, it's about Terry as well, he went to prison because of me.'

'No he didn't, he went to prison because he was stupid.'

'But he blamed me and now he wants the chance to finish it.'

'You're doing this for him?'

'Yeah.'

'Well don't expect me to wipe away your blood this time.'

'As if.'

'It makes no sense.'

'No, you're right, it doesn't make sense but I have to do it before I go.'

'Before you go? Go where?'

'Later.' Harry says then makes to turn around.

'Is there a problem Harry?' Charlie is suddenly behind him.

'Ah no Charlie, everything's fine.' Harry looks flustered.

'Don't lie to me, I trust you and I knew there was something wrong during the drive back here. Now I've overheard what Rita was talking about with Terry, what is going on with you two and what is he calling you out for?'

Harry sighs and tells Charlie the whole story.

46.

The rest of the wake went off without a hitch, Terry and his crew managed to avoid Harry and his most of the time. Rita barely spoke to Harry for the rest of the day, their closeness at their son's graveside had been spoiled by the revelation of the proposed encounter with Terry. She was also concerned about what he meant by his last statement.

Gradually the mourners dwindled away leaving just Harry's Mod crew, Charlie, Rita and Sara who all mucked in to clear up. All the plates and utensils had been packed into her car along with the small amount of leftover food.

Rita bought everyone, including Harry, a drink for their help.

'I suppose I'd better take you home.' Rita says to Harry.

'I'd appreciate that.' Harry replies, 'Charlie is staying at mine tonight, I'll run him back to his mum's on the scooter in the morning.'

'Humph.' Is all Rita could say as she picked up her bag and turned to leave the pub.

They drove in silence back to Harry's house, when they arrive back inside Rita turned to Charlie.

'Can you give us a bit of space Charlie?'

'Ah yeah sure, I'll go into the garage and polish the scooter.'

'Thanks honey.'

Charlie goes into the garage and in a few moments The Who starts to blast out from the CD player.

'Well?' Rita turns to face Harry with her arms tightly wrapped around her breasts with a look of thunder. 'Before you go where?'

'Sit down Reet,' Harry calmly responds, Rita doesn't move but just drums the fingers from her right hand on her left elbow. 'Please, just sit down will you?' Harry sighs, 'it's not good news.'

Rita's expression softens, going from anger to concern as she unfolds her arms to sit on the sofa. Harry sits on the arm and takes her hands and a deep breath.

'I've got liver cancer.'

Rita gasps as she puts her hands to her mouth to stifle a cry. Tears begin to well up in her eyes.

'How lo.......' The words are lost in her throat as she starts to cry.

'How long have I got? Not sure, doc didn't want to commit himself until I have more tests.'

'What about a transplant, chemo?'

'Too late, it's spreading to the rest of my body.'

'Are you in pain?'

'Yeah, a bit, I'm on some super-duper pain killers that I shouldn't be drinking with, but what's it going to do, kill me?'

Rita leans over quickly to throw her arms around him as her body heaves with sobs.

'Didn't think you'd care.'

Rita slaps him, not hard but enough to make her point.

'You bloody idiot! Just because we're not married anymore doesn't mean I don't care about you. What are you going to do?'

'I don't know, I don't want to end up like Ed, floating away on a cloud of morphine until it finally sees me off. I was hoping to go out in a blaze of glory.' With that Harry starts to laugh and Rita gives him another playful slap.

'I can nurse you, mop your brow and feed you through a tube.' Rita says trying to make light of the situation.

'What, and wipe my arse as well? No, thanks but no thanks.'

'You can't just give up.'

'Why not?'

'Because that's not you, it's not what you do.'

'Well maybe it is this time.'

'Don't you dare give up Harry York, I need you.'

'No you don't, not anymore. We had eleven wonderful years together until we lost Robbie. Then for the next five years I ruined your life and broke your heart a hundred times over with the drinking and moping about. I can't do that again.'

'And you think your dying is not going to break my heart again?'

'Maybe. Oh I don't know, I just didn't really think you would be that affected by it.'

'You're unbelievable, how could you possibly think that? We might have had a strained relationship in the last year or so of our marriage but it got much better after we divorced and we've been close friends for many years now, haven't we?'

Rita grabs both his hands again and clutches them to her chest.

'I don't want to lose you Harry but if that is what is going to happen I want to spend as much of the time that you have left with you.'

'In what way?'

'I don't know yet you'll have to give me a few days to think about it but I'll come up with a plan.'

'Ah! A Rita plan.' Harry's eyes widen as he smiles at the thought, 'I remember Rita plans, like the one you had when we bought our first flat.'

Rita laughs as she remembers the day they moved in.

'Oh Jeez, we hardly had a pot to piss in, just needed three hundred pounds for the deposit, to get a ninety five percent mortgage.'

'Sounds like peanuts these days.' Harry replies.

'It is, but it was a small fortune then, can you imagine? The flat was six grand, I mean six grand, I wonder what is worth now?' Rita muses.

'I did see it up for sale a few years ago, for, wait for it, three hundred and fifty grand.' Harry says then bursts out laughing to be joined by Rita.

'Pity we didn't keep it.' Rita adds.

'Yeah, isn't hindsight such a wonderful thing?' Says Harry

'I think Charlie has been polishing that scooter long enough now don't you think?' Rita says wiping the tears from her eyes, Harry nods in agreement, 'I'll be making tracks.'

'OK I'll pop into the café after I drop him home tomorrow, have the coffee on.'

'And a bacon sarnie?'

'And a bacon sarnie.'

Rita smiles and gently touches her hand to his cheek before standing on tip toes to kiss him softly on the lips.

'I love you Rita.'

'I know and I love you too, in a way.'

'Please, don't feel sorry for me.'

'I'll try not to, can't guarantee it though, but I will feel sorry for myself, it's really going to hurt.'

With that she goes to the garage door and shouts out to Charlie.

'Bye Charlie, see you soon, give my regards to your mother.'

Charlie quickly opens the door.

'Bye Rita.' He looks questioningly from her to Harry and back again but says nothing more. Rita smiles and waves to both of them then makes her way to the front door and leaves.

Charlie comes back into the house.

'Have you two kissed and made up?'

'Kind of.'

'You two were married once then.'

'We were,'

'I should have realised, the way you were with each other.'

'Yeah, I told you about the fight with Terry when he gave me the scar? Well it was Rita who stepped in and stopped it going any further, it all progressed from there.'

'And what went wrong?' Charlie asked him.

'Our son died, that's what went wrong and she handled it better than me. I just went completely off the rails. Drank too much and generally made her life hell before she eventually had enough and left me.'

'But you seem so close now.'

'We are, took a while for me to see the light, but when I did it was too late for us. Thankfully we managed to rebuild a friendship.'

'Is there no chance you can get back together? I can see she loves you very much.'

'Yeah but in a different way, almost like brother and sister now.'

'Is that what she says?'

'Sort of,'

'I wouldn't believe that.'

'Why, what would you know about it?' Harry seems defensive.

'Look, I'm sorry, maybe I don't know anything about it but I reckon she still loves you, no matter what she says, otherwise she wouldn't be the way she is with you. As an outsider, that's what I see.'

Harry looks thoughtful.

'You're quite perceptive for a kid.'

'I'm not a kid!'

Harry laughs and ruffles Charlie's hair.

'No mate, you're not.'

'What about this fight?'

'Ah yes, the fight.'

'I think you need a drink, then you can tell me all about it.'

47.

'Oh Harry, Harry.' Sara comes from behind the counter, racing to throw her arms around Harry as he comes through the door of Rita's café. She buries her face in his shoulder and starts to sob. Harry is embarrassed and looks over to Rita as he hesitantly puts his arms around Sara.

'You told her!' he mouths at Rita.

'Of course I told her, Rita replies, 'She's the closest we've got to a daughter, why wouldn't I tell her?'

Sara pecks Harry affectionately on the cheek, pulls back to look at him through her tears

'What exactly is it she told you?'

'The cancer,' Sara replies and stands back, 'Oh and about the punch up.'

'Maybe you should put a poster up?' Harry quips.

'You're being very brave, about the cancer I mean, the fight is just plain dumb.'

'Wise words Sara.' Harry replies.

'Come on, coffee and bacon sarnie time.' With that Sara skips off the kitchen to put the bacon on. Harry looks around for somewhere to sit and realises that it's almost full with most of the customers looking at him. He gives them a half smile and makes his way out to the kitchen where Rita has taken over from Sara who is now serving tables.

He sits on the chair in the corner.

'How you feeling today?' She asks him whilst affectionately touching his arm.

'Much the same as yesterday, a bit sad for Ed and Robbie, who'd have thought his funeral would be on the boy's birthday?'

'Yeah spooky.'

Sara pops in with his coffee.

'Thanks babe,' Harry says as she pops out again, Harry takes a sip and looks up to Rita who is cooking his bacon.

He takes a deep breath.

'I need you to do something for me.'

Rita removes the frying pan from the hob, sighs and looks round to face him.

'What now?'

'Charlie overheard about the fight, he wants to come to it as well.'

'WHAT! You can't be serious, he's just a kid. You, you can't involve him in your childish madness.'

'No! Harry asserts, 'no of course not, there's no way I want him to be involved but he knows when it will be.'

'And when is that?'

'This Sunday, midday, up where we were testing the scooter.'

'Who's going to be there?'

'Steve.'

'Why am I not surprised about that?' Rita interrupts, 'and I suppose Frank and Bernie as well?'

'Frank yes, but not Bernie, he didn't want to know.'

'So one of you has some sense.'

'Charlie wants to take his place. Of course I refused but he had already wormed out the time and date from me before declaring that he wanted to be there too.'

'I'll talk to him.'

'No, what I need you to do is be at my house Sunday morning, he thinks I'm going to take him up on the scooter. I'll already be gone. Steve's coming for me so you can keep him there till I get back.'

'What makes you so sure you'll be coming back?'

'Nobody's going to be killing anybody, it's just a...'

'Just a what? A fight? Like I said, it went well last time didn't it?'

'It's not like last time, I'm going to let Terry win so that he can save face and get over it'

'And what about your face?' Rita asks as she steps over to run her finger along his scar.

'Doesn't really matter now does it? I'm not going to be around long enough for it any difference to me.'

'I still think this is ridiculous, like a bunch of schoolboys fighting in the playground.'

'If it makes Terry feel better about himself then so be it, he's giving Charlie a job so I owe him. That brings me to something else.'

Rita rolls her eyes as if to say 'what now?'

'I want to leave the house to Charlie and his mother, and my scooter. Do you mind?'

'That's really sweet of you, of course I don't mind, are you sure?'

'Well, I had been going to leave it to you but since I've known them I felt they needed it more than you do. If they don't want to live so close to his father they can sell up and buy something else.'

'No I don't need it, I've got the café and the flat, that's not to mention all the money I was left. So yes, please leave it to Charlie, I'll keep an eye on them don't you worry about that. Anyway that's not going to happen for a long time, is it?'

159

'If only.'

'No, you are going back to the doctors, this time I'm coming with you, and if there is any chance that chemo can help then you're going to do it.'

'I don't know Reet, I told you, I don't want to end up like Ed.'

'I'm not going to let you give up.'

'Why?'

'Because I love you, you stupid bastard.'

With that she kisses him hard.'

'But you said….'

'Yeah I know, but it's a woman's prerogative to change her mind isn't it?'

Harry Laughs.

'I guess so.'

Rita finishes making his bacon sandwich and hands it to him.

'Thanks,' Henry mutters, 'for everything, not just the sarnie.'

'It's not a problem, I'm always here for you.' She hesitates for a few moments. 'However, I do wish you would give up on this fight, you're not well enough.'

'I'm not that bad at the moment, anyway, as I said before, I'll take a fall early, so he can win.'

'Make sure you do.' Harry says nothing more, 'I mean it Harry, take a few punches then fake a knockout.'

'That's what I'll do, fake a knock out.'

48.

Sunday morning was much like any other Sunday morning. People were having a late breakfast with their families, reading the Sunday rags with all the supplements and maybe a free DVD or CD to entertain them in the afternoon. Once upon a time in Britain there wasn't much else to do. TV didn't start till after lunch and all the shops, except newsagents, were shut, even then you couldn't buy much, maybe a porn magazine, well very soft porn, tits and bums really, but you couldn't buy a Bible, how did that ever make sense?

Sunday lunchtime was a ritual, the men would go to the pub, which only opened for two hours from midday till two. A crowd would be waiting outside for the magic hour when the landlord would shoot the bolt to let them in. Within a matter of minutes the pub would be heaving as the crowd fought for a place at the bar to get their round in. While the men folk were supping as many pints as possible in that short time, before driving home in the days before the breathalyser, the women were cooking the Sunday roast.

That's all in the past, these days the pubs are open all day with the majority being empty most of the time. All the shops are open which is where everyone is now, shopping malls, garden centres or DIY superstores.

That's progress for you.

On this particular Sunday the weather is sunny and cold, crisp and dry. Brighton's shops are doing a good trade, especially in the Lanes with the old soaks staring into their beer in whatever pubs are still trading.

This Sunday there is a knock at Harry's door and Rita opens it to Charlie.

'Hi Reet, is Harry ready?'

'Come in Charlie.' Rita stands aside to let him in, closes the door and sighs. 'No son, he's not.'

'Where is he?' Charlie looks concerned.

'Steve picked him up a while ago.'

'But I'm meant to be helping, taking part you know, one of the boys.'

'Yes I know.'

'I've got to go, I've got to help them.'

'Harry didn't want you to get involved.'

'But why not?'

'Come and sit down a moment, let me explain.'

Reluctantly Charlie takes a seat.

'I promised to be there.'

'I know you did, he told me. Look, this is an ancient feud going back to the day I met him. It's between Harry's old gang and Terry's, you weren't even thought of then.'

'But I'm young, I can really help.'

'Charlie, Harry had to eat a lot of humble pie to get Terry to take you on, how do you think he would react if you turned up to punch his lights out?'

'I don't care, Harry needs my help!'

'Well you should care, Harry cares about you more than you know. Why do you think he went to find your mother? Why did he ask Terry to take you on? Huh?'

Charlie looks sheepishly at the floor.

'I… I don't understand.'

'Our son died years ago, leukaemia, he sees you as our lost son, he wants you to have a good life and not to ruin it by getting involved in this piece of childishness. Trust me, this won't be a serious fight, a couple of bruises and it'll be all over and they'll be down the pub.'

'Do you really believe that Reet?'

'I have to Charlie,'

'And what if they don't end up in the pub together? Are you sure Harry's not hoping Terry will finish off the job he started all those years ago?'

'What do you mean?'

'Are you sure he doesn't want Terry to kill him?'

'Don't be daft, why would he?'

'I know he's got cancer, I heard him tell you the other night.'

'Yes he does but I'm going to make him do the chemo, what else did you hear?'

'Something about the house.'

'Yes he wants you and your mum to have it, and his scooter, when you've got a licence to ride it that is.'

'Don't you see it? He's putting his house in order so he can commit suicide by using Terry to do it.'

'No, he wouldn't be so…..'

'So what? Stupid? Or is it clever? Is he insured? If he committed suicide they wouldn't pay out, however, if he was murdered or killed accidentally, they would.'

Rita doesn't say anything, Charlie can see her turning it all over in her head until she suddenly stands up.

'Come on, let's hope we're not too late.'

Charlie looks gob smacked as Rita grabs her coat and keys to head for the door. As she swings it open she looks back at Charlie.

'Well, are you coming or not? You were dead keen five minutes ago?'

'Ah yes, of course but….'

'We've got to stop it!'

****

Meanwhile, on the other side of town, Harry, Steve and Frank have been joined by another four mods that Steve had managed to enlist to make up the numbers. Thankfully, depending on your point of view, the sun was shining, with no rain on the horizon. There was just the seven mods sitting on their scooters, some of them, including Harry, were smoking, patiently awaiting the arrival of the leather clad gang of bikers.

'They're late.' Steve points out.

'Fashionably late,' Harry adds.

'I still can't believe Bernie didn't want to come along.' Frank mutters.

'Yeah, yellow bastard.' Steve growls, 'and I thought I knew him, only goes to show.

'No, I respect his decision.' Says Harry. 'I wouldn't want to force him into doing anything he didn't want to.'

'Still, I....' Steve let his voice trail off. 'Never mind, we're here, that's all that matters.'

'Hey Steve, who's that coming up the lane?' One of the extra mods calls out, 'It's another scooter, not a bike.'

Everyone looks in that direction.

'There's a car coming up behind as well.' Steve adds.

'Well I'll be....' Frank exclaims whilst running his fingers through what was left of his hair. 'I don't fucking believe it, it's Bernie and after all he said about not wanting to get involved.'

'The trouble is, the car is Rita,' Harry mutters, 'and I'm willing to bet she's not alone.'

'Who else?' Franks asks him.

'Charlie, just who I didn't want to be here.'

'Surely Rita hasn't brought him to be part of this?' Steve asks him.

'Hmm good point, probably not, so the only other reason would be to try and stop me, us that is.'

'Can they?'

'Too late for that now, look who else is on the horizon.' Harry points to the dust being kicked up by the group of motorcycles coming in the distance.

Bernie arrives first to dismount and kick in the stand. He removes his crash helmet as Harry and co walk over to him.

'We thought you.....' Steve starts to say.

'Didn't want to be involved.' Bernie answers for him, 'no, I don't, I still think this is daft but we've been friends a long time and I couldn't live with myself if something bad happens to you lot while I'm at home with my feet up.'

'Well it won't be long now, here they come.' Frank points out.

'Let me deal with Rita first.' Harry says as he moves away to greet Rita and Charlie who have now pulled up and alighted from the car.

'Harry, Harry, you've got to stop this.' Rita pleads breathlessly as she runs to meet him.

'What are you doing here and why did you bring Charlie? I specifically asked to you keep him at home.' Harry asks angrily.

'Because we know what you're up to!' Rita replies, just as angrily.

'What do you mean?' Harry pulls back with a frown.

'You want Terry to kill you, so you don't have to commit suicide and the insurance will pay out.'

Harry starts to laugh.

'Are you serious?'

Rita starts to look embarrassed.

'Er yes I am, I mean I was.'

Harry puts his arms around her, still laughing.

'No, I'm not getting Terry to kill me, I wouldn't do that to him. I told you I'm going to take a fall.' He pulls back, and beckons Charlie, who is looking worried, to come closer. He puts a hand on each of their shoulders.

'Harry?' Charlie looks questioningly at him.

'Look, I'm going to do the chemo, doc says it might work. It might not but I've got you two and that makes me a lucky man. So I have to try.'

'Oh Harry!' Rita throws her arms around his neck and kisses him full and hard on the lips. 'I just....'

'It's okay babe, it's okay.'

'Come on Harry, I'll stand with you.' Charlie says.

'No you won't, you'll stand and watch. It'll be a bit like when there's a re-enactment of the Battle of Hastings, not serious, just a bit of fun.

Charlie looks unconvinced, Harry smiles and ruffles his hair.

'Really?' Charlie asks.

'Really.' Harry replies.

Terry and the bikers had pulled up about fifty yards away from the mods, he is still straddling his bike when Harry looks over and nods.

'I'm just going for a quick parley with the leader of the gang, you lot wait here.'

'You sue you'll be okay?' Steve asks him.

'Yeah, no worries.' With that he gives Rita a quick peck on the lips, ruffles Charlie's hair once more, and walks over to Terry.

'Be careful Harry.' Charlie calls after him, Harry looks back over his shoulder without stopping and smiles.

'Good turn out today Harry.' Terry states as Harry comes up close to him.

'Yeah, weather's on our side as well, would have been shit had it been raining.'

'You're right there.' Terry replies.

'You still up for this?' Harry asks him.

'Why, aren't you?'

'Sure I am, just wanted to check you weren't chickening out.'

Terry starts to laugh.

'Not me matey, I'm a Rocker and Rockers don't chicken out, ever. Even though it looks like you've got a larger contingent that we have.' Terry says indicating Bernie, Harry looks over towards him.

'He wasn't expected, I'll ask him to sit it out, and he didn't want to be involved in the first place.'

'Nah, don't worry, we'd thrash you even if you had half a dozen more.'

This time Harry laughs.

'In your dreams Terry, in your dreams.' They look at each other in silence for a few minutes. 'Only fists, no chains, bats of any kind,' Harry pauses for a few seconds. 'Or knives.' With that he touches his scar.'

'Only fists, just give the word.'

'What about Pete?' Harry asks Terry.

'I took him to the police, the old lady is recovering so it's only the mugging and the fact that he came in voluntarily will go in his favour. Thanks again for the heads up.'

'No problem.'

Harry turns and goes back to the other Mods who are standing waiting.

Harry and Terry lock eyes.

Epilogue – The March of the Mod

Today the sun is shining on the coastal town of Brighton. The Mods and Rockers clashes of the past are just that, a thing of the past, relegated to history. Unlike the days before film there are many scenes to be viewed, (especially on YouTube) of the clashes of the sixties. Today Brighton is a bustling town that still draws huge crowds during the holiday periods, and the weekend.

It's more than a year since Edward Rawlings was buried with full honours by his family and friends, a time well remembered by all who were there.

Today most of those present at Ed's funeral are there for another one.

Today they are there to pay their respects to Harold Albert York who had finally succumbed to liver cancer, after a brave battle against it.

Charlie was dressed immaculately in his Zoot Suit, looking every inch the Mod Harry had been back when he had been the lad's age. Now over a year older than when Harry had first met him, he was even more mature and Harry would probably have said more mature than he had been at that age. Having now turned sixteen Charlie had his licence to ride a scooter, although he hadn't arrived on it today.

This time he came with Rita, his mother, and his father in the lead car.

Harry would have seen the irony in the person who gave the eulogy for him.

Terry.

'If Harry is looking down on us now he must be laughing uncontrollably. As most of you here know it was me who gave him his famous scar way back in the seventies. He was a good man, to be honest I didn't know him that well until the last year when I took on his young charge Charlie Conrad. Charlie is a good lad who I am hoping will eventually take over my garage, and I have Harry to thank for that.

'I also have to thank Harry's wife and widow, Rita, who stopped me killing him back in the day, when Harry and I were a lot younger and lot more stupid. I'm going to miss him. I wish we had been friends a lot longer than we were. I wish I hadn't nearly killed him or given him his famous scar, but I'm glad we met.

'He saved my grandson from going completely off the rails and I'm sincerely grateful for that as well. All in all Harry York was one of the best, who is now riding around somewhere with his old mate Ed Rawlings.

'I remember something he said at Ed's funeral that I think is as true today as it was then. To be seen, stand up; to be heard, speak up; to be appreciated, shut up. So that is what I will do and thank Harry for being Harry.'

Harry had told Rita what music he wanted for his funeral. He really would have liked The Jam but felt that Ed had done that so had chosen 'Itchycoo Park' and 'Tin Soldier' by The Small Faces. He had also requested that the mourners not dress in black, anything but. Rita, however, did dress in black.

Harry hadn't any religious beliefs so there had not been any kind of religious ceremony. He had asked to be cremated and after the coffin had disappeared behind the doors the crowd made their way outside to view whatever flowers had been sent. Harry had asked people not to spend money on flowers but to donate the money to one of the cancer charities.

All the mourners gathered around Rita to offer their condolences which she accepted gratefully.

'I'm really going to miss him Rita.' Charlie came to speak to her, putting his arms around her neck. 'I just can't believe he's gone.'

'Neither can I Charlie, he's been part of my life for over forty years, through thick and thin.'

'It was so wonderful when you two got married again, such a great day.'

'Yes it was, but he was fading fast on that day, did his best to put on a brave face but he was in considerable pain.'

'But you were there for him and I will always love you for that.'

'Thank you Charlie.' Rita says as she puts her arm around his neck. 'So, how are things with you and your parents?'

'Couldn't be better.' came Chrissie's voice from behind, making Rita turn around to face her.

'Chrissie, so glad you could come, how are you doing?'

'Well, as you know, Harry left his house to me and Charlie, I didn't know until a few days ago. Charlie did but kept it to himself until Harry died. I am really overwhelmed by it.'

'It's what we wanted. Harry and I felt like Charlie was our son. You know we lost ours when he was quite young.'

'Yes Charlie told me.'

'I see your ex is here today as well.'

'Yes, he is a new man, again thanks to Harry. Oh we're not getting back together but we do have an understanding.'

'I'm glad to hear it, and I am sure Harry would be as well.'

With that Chrissie takes Rita's hand briefly before turning away from her, leaving Charlie at her side.

'I'm happy for you and your mum' Rita says to Charlie.

He hugs her once more.

Rita looks around to the people there. Steve and the gang trying to look cheerful, but failing miserably as they chat with Terry and his gang.

Half a dozen drivers from the bus company.

Inspector Lewis and a contingent from Brighton police.

Sara with her current boyfriend, she had cried so much in the café when Harry had finally gone. This new man was a good one Rita told her.

But don't marry him she thought to herself with a quiet smile.

THE END

AFTERWORD

In 2017 I was sent a script by Stephen M. Smith entitled Mods, we had worked together on a film of my book 'Two's Up' which was renamed 'Borstal'. The idea was that I would write a novelisation of the script to coincide with the film. To be honest the script wasn't very good but I liked idea having grown up with the original 60's mod erea. Had I just written something based on the script it would have been a very short story. So I took some elements and characters and created a completely different story which is what you have just read.

I'd like to thank Terry Rawlings who is *'The'* expert on all things Mod, check out his book – 'Mod: Clean Living Under Very Difficult Circumstances – A Very British Phenomenon' and his book on the death of Brian Jones – 'Who Killed Christopher Robin', for his tweaking of the 'March of the Mods' introduction.

I would also like to thank my old, old friend Sheila Machray for proof reading, so any mistakes still there are her fault! LOL.

Finally love and thanks to my wife Ziggy who is happy for me to lock myself away creating something be it music or literature (is this novel literature?)

I am always interested to hear from readers, opinions welcome kris@krisgray.co.uk

Information on 'Two's Up' www.twos-up.com

Thank you all so much.
Kris Gray Germany 2019

Printed in Great Britain
by Amazon

63804186R00097